The Adventures of Henry Woods, Life in Early Texas

MYSTERY AT THE OLD STONE FORT

BOOK THREE

PAUL N. SPELLMAN

Dedication

This book is dedicated to the 1995 7th Grade Class at Tuloso-Midway Independent School District. It is my hope that this story provided them with a meaningful and engaging narrative, crafted especially for their enjoyment and inspiration.

Table of Contents

About the Author

Paul N. Spellman is an historian, author, and speaker, retiring in 2023 as Professor of Texas and U.S. History after more than thirty years teaching at the secondary and university level. With degrees from Southwestern University, The University of Texas, and a PhD from the University of Houston, he is the author of more than a dozen published books on Texas History, many available on Kindle and Audio Books as well as in print.

Spellman has now added this five-book series for young teens and families, **The Adventures of Henry Woods; Life in Early Texas**, and is working on a 2025 writing project as well.

Dr. Spellman is a sought-after speaker across Texas. He and his wife Kathleen live along the Brazos River in Richmond, Texas

Historical Introduction

In the late eighteenth century, the northern provinces of Spanish-held Mexico seemed much too distant from Mexico City for many settlers to even think about living there. It was a hostile world, with a desert climate and roving Indians, and no Spanish *presidio* to protect those who would dwell there.

One of the brave leaders who took people into Texas was Gil Y'Barbo, settling his people between the Neches and Sabine Rivers. Y'Barbo built a stone fort there, and the town of Nacogdoches eventually grew up around it.

The old stone fort in East Texas became a haven for many settlers as well as the headquarters for filibustering expeditions in the early 1800s. Philip Nolan's men were kept as prisoners there after the death of their leader. The Gutierrez-Magee Expedition passed through the area, and James Long used the fort as his new republic's capital.

As the *empresarios* moved their colonies into Texas during the 1820s, Nacogdoches became one of the permanent sites for travelers from the United States. Peter Ellis Bean, a survivor of earlier filibuster campaigns, commanded an outpost of soldiers at the fort, although he was unpopular with both Anglo and Mexican settlers in the area.

In 1827, Haden and Benjamin Edwards tried to establish an independent republic in Texas named Fredonia. Their headquarters were in the old stone fort. Even after the Fredonian Rebellion had been suppressed by the Mexican army, others plotted similar uprisings in and around Nacogdoches.

By 1830, Nacogdoches had become a thriving community and the main point of entry along the Sabine. Settlers from all over North America and Europe lived there. The Thomas Rusk family lived there, and Sam Houston moved there late in 1832.

Trouble brewed during those years, with suspicious activities of the nearby American Indians as well as those of the Texans themselves. When the Texas Revolution erupted in October 1835, the people of Nacogdoches played an important role.

In the summer of 1835, only weeks before the conflict at Gonzales, the east Texas town was a busy commercial center crowded with visitors and merchants from all over Texas trading and debating the heated issues of the day. Behind the public scene, high drama concealed itself in the shadows of plots and conspiracies. At the center of this intrigue stood Vicente Cordova, a man of mystery and danger who would ignite an uprising among the Cherokee in 1838.

All of the characters in this story are based on actual people who lived in Texas during the colonial days. Zadock and Minerva Cottle Woods had lived in Texas since 1824. They had several children, including Henry Gonsalvo, their youngest. His friends in this story, Crooked Path, Antonio, and Marisol, are fictional but represent the many young people who grew up amidst the danger and excitement of the Texas frontier.

Legend and myth still surround the Old Stone Fort, which stands today in the center of the Stephen F. Austin State University campus.

PROLOGUE

The mountain lion crept to the edge of the precipice and looked down on its unsuspecting prey. A tiny shower of pebbles cascaded down the canyon wall as the big gray cat's front paws grasped the edge. Its front legs bent slightly, and the stalking hunter instinctively measured the distance of the leap down into the small box canyon. Piercing yellow eyes stared at the victim as it moved quietly across the canyon floor. The hungry cat became motionless, its pointed ears flattened back against its head. Only a moment until the attack would begin. The lion tightened its muscles in readiness.

Marisol unbuttoned her brightly-colored skirt, unwrapped it from her waist, and laid it on the flat-topped boulder beside her bodice. She stepped lightly out of her leather sandals and glanced around the canyon. She had come alone as always, but she looked around shyly anyway. Over in the middle of the canyon, the pond formed from a natural spring beckoned to her. The teenage girl walked quickly across to the edge of the deep pool, her arms crossed in front of her. She tested the water with her toes: It was cold even on this hot August day and felt good in contrast to the sun that beat down from overhead.

Marisol stopped when she heard the noise behind her and turned around to see the small rocks strike the ground at the bottom of the canyon wall. Looking up to see what had started the tiny landslide, she stared directly into the sun. Shading her eyes with one hand, she could barely make out a strange gray shape silhouetted by the noonday sun.

The mountain lion snarled as it sprang from the edge, lunging straight down in a fluid, frightening motion. Its front claws extended out like knife blades pointed at the girl's throat. Only an instant remained before the cat's full weight crushed its prey to the ground.

Marisol threw her arms back behind her at the same moment the big cat sprang from its perch above. Her feet slipped on the wet banks of the pond and she stumbled in a rough cartwheel into the water. Even as the water erupted in a splash, the girl had straightened her arms and legs in full extension as she dove beneath the surface.

The *puma* hit the ground hard, having missed its prey, and rolled onto its side for just a second. Quickly regaining its balance on all fours, it let out a growl of frustration and prepared to pounce again. But the girl had disappeared. The water rippled in front of the cat as it waited for her to resurface.

Marisol descended beneath the safety of the dark waters, pulling with long practiced strokes until she had come to the middle of the pond. The last of the breath in her lungs gone, she forced herself upward until her hands and head broke the surface. Inhaling quickly, she managed a brief glance back at her pursuer. The cat stood at the edge of the pool glaring in her direction.

But instead of going back under, Marisol treaded water where she had surfaced, calling on all of her courage to stare right back into the ugly yellow eyes of the cat. For several seconds hunter and hunted captured each other in a deadly stare. Marisol felt chills climb up her spine: was it the cold spring water or just the fear racing through her?

The cat broke off its stare, glanced once down at the water's edge, and sprang out over the pool, splashing clumsily as it struck the surface. Its front legs began paddling immediately as it labored to keep its head above the water. It flicked water from its ears as it made its way slowly toward its prey.

Less than fifteen feet separated the two swimmers. Wait, Marisol told herself silently, not yet. Not yet. One more second. *Now!* She twisted her hips and shoulders in one movement until she faced away from the approaching enemy, reaching forward with her arms and calling on all of her strength as she began to swim. All the hours of swimming in this pond and the river nearer her home helped in the next few seconds as she began to increase the distance from her attacker.

Eight strokes, ten and eleven. Her feet struck the bottom of the pond as she reached the shallow edge. She scrambled up out of the water, never looking back as she broke into a run across the canyon and onto the familiar path.

The mountain lion never saw the girl running. It had already turned around and begun to paddle to the muddy edge it had just left.

There would be another hunt. And soon: the cat was very hungry.

CHAPTER ONE

"Ouch!" Marisol winced and cried out from the pain shooting through her ankle.

"I'm sorry, Marisol," Antonio pulled his hand back from her ankle. "I was just trying to help."

"I know," she replied gently. "Thank you, Tonio. But my leg hurts, and it's swollen and - Mama?"

"*Si?* "Señora Calderon answered as she stood beside her daughter's bed.

"Is my ankle broken, do you think?"

"No," her mother said with a smile. "It is very badly sprained, but not broken. You will have to stay off of it for several days, perhaps."

"Several days?" Marisol said with surprise. "But Mama, what about the trip? Will I be able to go on the trip?"

"We will have to see, my darling," Señora Calderon replied as she reached to pull the blanket up over the girl's leg. Tonio stood up from where he had been kneeling beside his girlfriend, moving out of the way as her mother straightened the pillows and patted her daughter gently on the cheek.

"Don't worry, Marisol," Tonio whispered after Señora Calderon had left the room. "We will all take care of you so that you can go with us. I will take care of you myself," he added. The teenage girl smiled weakly.

"Thank you, Tonio," she said. "I don't want to be left behind."

Henry held his breath and waited. He lay on his stomach in the middle of the long grassy prairie he knew so well as his own backyard. The brown late summer sawgrass waved gently all around him, camouflaging the boy as he hid expectantly. He had pulled his wide-brimmed hat down over his forehead, and his arms extended on the soft ground in front of him. In his right hand, he held one end of a string made from the tendons of a whitetail deer. The string wound across the ground for five feet, ending in a loop that Henry had fashioned. The loop lay over a hole.

Henry kept his eyes glued on the gopher hole in front of him. Beads of sweat rolled down the back of his neck and dropped into the soil. His left ear itched but the silent hunter tried to ignore it. He dared not budge for fear of frightening the pesky rodent that lay just beneath the surface. If he waited long enough, and quietly enough, the critter would stick its head out and right into Henry's trap, and then -

Two brown ears emerged from the hole, then the top of the gopher's head. It faced away from Henry. Good, he thought to himself, just one more second. Henry tightened his fingers around the string and counted silently to himself: *one, two, three, pull!* The loop closed quickly around the prairie animal's neck just below its tiny chin. Henry rose up on his left elbow and to his knees as he jerked the trap toward him. The gopher squealed as it was wrenched from its hovel, its sharp claws pawing the air as it tumbled onto the ground. Henry sat back on his haunches and pulled a second time.

But the gopher had not given up trying to escape the deadly snare. It twisted onto its feet and faced the boy who held the string. Instead of pulling against the choking noose, the furry animal charged right at him. Henry's eyes widened in surprise as the critter headed for him. He tried to stand but he lost his balance and began to fall over on his back. He clutched the string as he fell, his legs splayed out wide. Henry raised his head awkwardly and looked down the length of his sprawling body.

The gopher scuttled across the prairie ground, its little legs spinning like wheels. It made a desperate dash right up onto Henry's stomach and leapt for his head. Henry squeezed his eyes shut as the gopher planted its four clawed feet on his face and launched itself into the air. Henry let go of the string and grabbed his face in pain. He rolled over onto his stomach and peeked through his fingers.

The gopher ran in a straight line through the brown grass, bouncing out of sight, the looped string snare trailing behind it as it disappeared.

Henry sat up on his knees and drew his hands from his face. Drops of blood mixed with dirt and perspiration stained the palms of both hands. But the pain had already gone and he knew there would be no serious damage.

The teenager stood up, brushed his homespun pants with his hands, and then wiped his face with his shirt sleeve.

"Shoot!" he shouted in disgust.

"Next time try a smaller animal," came a voice from off to Henry's left. He wheeled around to see who had hollered. Tonio Gonzalez, Henry's best friend, sat on his horse, one leg looped easily over the saddle horn. As Henry started to speak, the Tejano boy reared back his head and let out a long, whooping laugh, slapping his side with his black ten-gallon hat.

"How long have you been watching?" Henry knew better than to ask.

"Saw the whole thing," Tonio answered, suddenly frowning seriously. "You were so brave," he said in a low voice. "That big dangerous monster came right out of its dark cave and you stood your ground. Well, I guess you sat on your ground. I was very impressed." Tonio emphasized *very*.

"Never mind," Henry said, brushing himself off once more. "I never thought the thing would come right at me." As if to end the whole ordeal, Henry reached down for a clod of dirt and heaved it in the general direction of the long-departed gopher. Henry shook his head and turned back to

Tonio. "What are you doing here, anyway? I thought you were coming Saturday with your family."

"We're still coming," Tonio replied as he urged his horse into a slow walk toward Henry. "But my father asked me to bring a message to the fort: said it was *muy importante.* "

"My parents are at home, and Norman's over, too," Henry said. "Give me a lift up." Tonio guided the roan mare to meet Henry, who grabbed a helping arm as he slid onto the horse's rump. "Let's ride."

Tonio glanced over his shoulder at his best friend. "Hold on tight now," he said with a smile. "That monster could be anywhere."

"Oh shut up."

CHAPTER TWO

"Colonel Austin's back in Texas?" Henry Woods blurted out. The men standing on the front porch turned and stared at the teenager in surprise. Henry's face reddened in embarrassment: boys were not to speak around the adults unless spoken to. "I'm sorry," he stammered as he hung his head.

"That's all right, son," Mr. Robinson said. "We're all startled by the news. Colonel Austin has been gone for nearly two years. Some had given up hope of ever laying eyes on him again."

"True enough, James," Henry's father added. "Some of us figured him for dead in a Mexican prison until we heard different last fall." Zadock Woods grinned slyly. "We almost went down there after him."

The three men laughed and nodded at that statement. Men like Zadock Woods, James Cummings, and Ben Milam never waited for anything very patiently. These frontiersmen preferred action to words, and some had called for an expedition into Mexico back in 1834, to rescue Stephen Austin. Only the deadly cholera epidemic had kept them home.

"Anyway, that's the report I've come to deliver," Robinson said. "Austin's ship landed in New Orleans just a week or so ago, and he's riding over right now."

"Where's he headed?" the third man asked. Lieutenant James Cummings had served as Austin's official back when the first colonists arrived.

"I expect he'll head home, to San Felipe," Robinson replied. "Then he'll go up to Washington, maybe Nacogdoches, too."

Nacogdoches, Henry thought to himself. That's where we're headed in a few days! Maybe I could meet Mr. Austin there. What an honor that would be.

"It will be an interesting time for all of us," Zadock said. "Lot of confusion around here. Some want war, others do not. Austin's opinion is mighty high on everyone's list."

"You're right about that, Zadock," Robinson said with a nod of his head. "Bill Wharton is calling for a war, and there's a lot of support for it. If Austin's changed his mind and comes over to the war hawks, plenty of folks will load up."

"Count me in," Zadock said quickly. Henry smiled as he listened to his father. "I fought the Sac and Fox in Illinois and the Creeks with Andy Jackson. We took on the lobster backs at New Orleans and the Comanche right out there in my own backyard." Zadock pointed for emphasis. "I'll fight the Mexicans if I have to. Old Santy Ana can just bring the whole army up here to the prairie. Jim Robinson, you and me can lick 'em before dinner."

Everyone laughed at the speech, even Zadock himself. The sixty-two-year-old settler from Massachusetts had seen a lifetime full of fighting and surviving. That was life on the frontier. There was always plenty of time for bragging, but when family and home were on the line, it became serious business for those who would stand to protect what belonged to them.

"Where you headed now, Lieutenant?" Robinson asked.

"Going on over to Moore's Ferry," he replied, motioning off to the east. "I just came up from Gonzales and I'm making my way east and then north."

"You need some help?" Zadock asked.

"Thanks, Mr. Woods, but we have several riders spreading the word."

Cummings tipped his hat in respect to the older man, shook hands with him and Robinson, waved at Henry and Antonio, and climbed back into the saddle. "Y'all take care now," he hollered over his shoulder as he rode across the prairie toward the Colorado River.

Henry and Tonio watched as he rode away. The two men walked back inside Zadock's home to talk over the news.

"You think there'll be war?" Tonio asked his friend as they leaned against the porch fence.

"Don't know," Henry said, his mind wandering in a daydream of battles and marching armies. "Father says we'll fight anyone who tries to take our land or our freedom."

"You think they'll let us fight?"

"Dunno," Henry mumbled, then brightened as he stood up straight. "I know one thing: if the Mexican army comes marching over that hill yonder " - he pointed to the west - "I'll stand right here and fight for my home."

"Brave words, *compadre*," Tonio answered with a grin. "You just better hope they aren't riding on gophers."

"Oh shut up."

CHAPTER THREE

"Henry!" His mother's voice echoed across the yard from the cookhouse.

"Yes, Mother!" he called back.

"Are you finished with the wagon and the horses?" Minerva Woods softened her voice when she realized her son was only a few steps away.

"Yes ma'am," Henry answered quickly. "The wagon is rigged up and nearly loaded. Horses, too."

"Go find your father then," she instructed as she turned to finish closing up the cooking room that sat just off the main house.

"Yes ma'am," he called over his shoulder. Henry dashed from the back fence around the house to the front. His father and oldest brother stood talking up by the front gate. The thick wooden gate swung open as it always did except when the signal of an Indian raid brought the nearby settlers inside the prairie fort. Then the Woods home became a *presidio* built to protect the families against attack.

"Father!" Henry shouted. Zadock Woods turned his head in the direction of the boy's voice. The old man's long white hair was ruffled from the prairie breeze that cooled this August morning. He watched as his youngest son ran up to his side.

"What's the hurry, son?" Zadock asked gently. "You have Comanches chasing you?" Norman, Henry's thirty-year-old brother, chuckled.

"Mama said it's time to finish loading the wagon for the trip," Henry said breathlessly, ignoring the remark about Indians.

"Well, son," Zadock drawled slowly, "why don't you go ahead and do just that? And while you're at it, rig up the team and bring the wagon round to the gate." The old man looked out across the prairie. "We'll be ready to go before Noon, I reckon." He paused for a moment in thought. "If the others get here sooner, we can make good time before sundown."

"I saw Tonio two days ago," Henry replied. "He said his family and the Calderons would be here right on time."

"Then I expect they will," Zadock nodded. "Mr. Gonzalez is a good man, a man of his word."

"Where do you think you'll camp tonight, Father?" Norman spoke up.

"Going to try to make the second ferry north, about twenty miles," Zadock answered.

"Pretty good trip with the children along," Norman suggested.

"What children?" Henry interrupted with a frown. "There won't be any children coming."

Norman smiled at his father, who winked back at him.

"No," said Norman, "'cept you and Tonio and Marisol, that is."

"Hey, you better take that back," Henry raised his voice, and one fist, defiantly. "I'm near sixteen, sixteen in the fall."

"Oh, please excuse me," Norman said in a mock tone of courtesy, bowing slightly at the waist. "Sixteen, my oh my, think of that, will you?"

Henry took a friendly swing at his brother. Norman eluded the mild punch, reached over, and tousled Henry's hair good-naturedly.

"Before you boys decide to go to war," their father spoke up as he watched, "why don't you finish your chore, Henry? You can take up with your brother when we come back."

"Norman, I sure wish you and Aunt Jane would come along," Henry had stepped back from the gate as his father spoke. "We'll be back in three weeks."

"I know, little brother," Norman replied. "But I've got two fields to turn under, and Monte has some cattle that need branding on his place."

"Go on now, son," Zadock said. "Get the wagon ready and tell your mother to send Wash around."

"Yessir." Henry ran back to the barn to finish rigging the two plow horses to the wagon. The wide-shouldered horses stood placidly alongside the wagon, nibbling at tufts of brown grass, their tails swishing the summer flies away. Henry led them by the bits until they stood in front of the wagon. The double rig lay on the ground, needing only to be

24

hoisted up and latched onto the wagon and tethered to the two horses.

As Henry worked, the sweat ran down his face and soaked into his gray cotton shirt. He paused to wipe the perspiration from his eyes, pulling the blue bandana out of his back pocket.

"Gulp of water, Mistah Henry?" Old Wash stood at the door at the side of the barn with a well bucket in his right hand.

"Thanks Wash," Henry said. "I'd be obliged."

The tall black man ambled over to the rig and offered Henry a tin cup dipped into the bucket of water. The cool water from the deep well by the house tasted wonderful to the boy as he finished off a second cup as quickly as the first.

"Want some help?" Wash asked in his quiet voice.

"Thanks," said Henry. The two worked together without speaking, both knowing exactly how to set the rig, having done the chore hundreds of times before. They finished in just a few minutes, and Old Wash disappeared behind the barn without another word said. Henry climbed up onto the wide wagon seat, grabbed the reins easily in his left hand, and gave them an expert jerk.

"C'mon, Sally," he hollered at the horse rigged on his left. The broad-backed mare snorted as she pulled hard. Next to her, the younger horse reacted a moment later, causing it to stumble just slightly when the shoulder rig pinched its haunches.

"Nicodemus, pay attention," Henry instructed as if the plow horse could understand. Henry guided the wagon slowly until it came alongside the side porch of the house. Pulling the reins until the wagon stopped, Henry jumped to the ground and reached for the boxes stacked nearby. He loaded the supplies and camp equipment on either side of the wagon bed, estimating the balance of the weight that would keep the wagon stable as they traveled.

Satisfied that his work was completed, Henry wiped his hands down the sides of his pants and stepped up on the side porch, cupping both hands around his mouth as he hollered:

"Wagon's loaded! Goin' to Nacogdoches!"

CHAPTER FOUR

The one-hundred-mile journey took five days and four nights. The four wagons and accompanying riders set an easy pace each morning just before dawn, stopping every few hours to water the livestock at stream crossings, and setting up camp just after sunset each evening.

They rode cross-country from Woods Prairie northwest until they came to the Camino Real, the old Spanish road that connected San Antonio and Nacogdoches with destinations south into Mexico. Never much more than a wagon-wide trail across the flatlands of central and east Texas, the King's Highway as it was often called provided the most direct route for traders, soldiers, and settlers to traverse the long distance between the Rio Grande and the Sabine.

Henry and Tonio rode together for most of the journey, usually at a short distance from the dusty trail of the wagons. Their duty consisted of watching for unfriendly Indians, especially just above the Colorado River crossing, and retrieving stray cattle that wandered off the road. The four families brought cattle to trade at the fair, enough to make a herd of about twenty. In addition, the Calderon prodded two large hogs along the trail, and six extra horses completed the caravan.

Zadock and Minerva Woods usually led the caravan in their wagon since Zadock had charge of selecting the evening campsites. Their son Norman and his wife Jane tagged along just behind, with the Gonzalez and Calderon families bringing up the rear. Marisol, Tonio's girlfriend, rode with her parents each morning but rode her own black mare in the afternoons. She helped Henry and Tonio chase down strays. Henry thought that the two of them were spending more time chasing each other while he looked after the cattle, but he didn't mind very much. He liked the time to himself riding through the mesquite and post oak, and daydreaming when there was nothing else to do.

The caravan crossed the Brazos River near Burnham's Crossing on the first day and turned northeast along the Camino Real after that. Ferrying barges assisted in the fording of the San Gabriel and the Navasota rivers on the second and third days.

Early on the last day of the trip, just as they came in sight of the Trinity River, Zadock pulled his wagon to a stop just off the side of the trail. Surrounding the caravan, tall pine, and fir trees stood as an army of sentinels, blocking the rays of the morning sun. The trail cut through a dense thicket here as it turned more to the east. The green pine forest marked quite a change from the rolling plains that skirted along the Colorado River and became Woods Prairie far now to the south.

Zadock pointed off to his left to a break in the thick woods. Henry and Tonio, both on horseback some fifty paces behind the wagons, squinted through the dawn mist in the direction he pointed. A clearing had been cut into the forest and what looked like the remnants of a settlement sat quietly in the shadows. Several buildings stood in various stages of disrepair. All the roofs had caved in. What had once been a corral now looked like a tornado had hit it. Broken barrels lay on their sides in what used to be yards, and over one broken-down building, a store's sign swung gently on its leather hinges.

But there was no sign of life anywhere. No animals wandered about, except for two raccoons that soon disappeared when they spotted the intruders from the road. No children played, no men or women walked out of the houses.

Henry and Tonio rode cautiously to the edge of the abandoned town. Henry peered inside one of the broken-down huts but did not get off of his horse. A crowded world of cobwebs covered the inside of the building as if someone had spent hours spinning cotton string and tossing it in odd, wheeling patterns everywhere. Behind him Tonio sat quietly on his mount, uneasy about being this close to such a strange place.

"What is this, Father?" Henry called over his shoulder back toward the wagons.

"Bucareli," Zadock answered in a voice just loud enough to be heard but with a strange tone to the word he spoke. Henry frowned.

"Buca- what?"

"Bucareli," Zadock repeated the word more slowly. "The old town of Gil Ybarbo," he began, "stood here along the Trinity many years ago, a thousand miles from civilization. Settlers came here without anyone to protect them from the Indians, without permission from their government. The settlers followed Ybarbo into the thicket, and named their town Bucareli." Zadock paused for effect. "Then the town shut down." Tonio's eyes widened. He looked around him.

"Folks just up and left," Zadock continued. "Crossed the Neches to the north, left their homes and stores behind."

"Why?" Henry asked, not wanting his father's story to end too soon.

"No one knows," Zadock replied with a sly grin. "Some say the thicket closed in on them, scared them away." The old man stroked his white beard in thought. "Some say the Indian ghost dance did it."

"Ghost dance?" Tonio couldn't help himself from interrupting. In the wagon behind Norman Woods, Tonio's father smiled at his wife.

"Yep," said Zadock. "An ancient medicine man, dead for a thousand years, spooked the people of Bucareli. Dancing on their houses at night, sent the wind inside closed doors. The moon turned red at night, and the sun disappeared for weeks at a time from the sky. Big blue sky, too."

"Where'd they go, Father?" Henry was caught up in his own imagination as he listened: huge ghost dancers and red moons leaped from housetop to housetop.

"Can't say," Zadock lowered his voice dramatically. "Some say they went all the way to the Sabine, others say Nacogdoches. The ghost dancers chased them out of the thicket, that's for sure."

The two boys sat in their saddles staring across the old settlement. Nothing moved for a moment. Then, out of nowhere, a breeze struck the edge of the forest, bending the small saplings in an eerie dancing motion. A red-tailed hawk rose from its high perch on a pine treetop and caught the breeze under its wings. Instinctively, both boys drew back on their reins, causing their mounts to step backward.

"Best be moving on from this ghost town, boys," Zadock called out to break the silence.

"Ghost town," Tonio shuddered under his breath. He turned the head of his mount and spurred it into a fast gait back onto the trail. Henry galloped right behind.

"Giddap, Nicodemus," Zadock urged the plow horse. The caravan worked itself back into motion along the eastern trail. Minerva Woods gently punched her husband in the side. Zadock smiled.

CHAPTER FIVE

The aging town of Nacogdoches bustled with the excitement of the autumn fair. People rode into the community from every direction, some from as far away as New Orleans and Mobile. Texans came from Houston and Galveston to the south and from San Antonio de Bexar and Gonzales. They came in long caravans of wagons and livestock, or alone on horseback. Friendly Cherokees from up the Angelina River traded at the fair, and several Tonkawa families had made their way from their village on the Brazos. They brought blankets and beads to trade for cotton fabrics, gunpowder, and oddities from the white man's village: top hats and bonnets, suspenders, and such.

Crooked Path wandered through the town fair on his own, keeping to himself whenever a crowd of Texans approached him. He wanted no trouble and seemed uncomfortable in these streets. But he loved to look at all of the things at the fair. Earlier in the day he had spotted a leather vest hanging from a hook in the window of one of the stores. Thin leather braids lined the edge of the vest, and a bright yellow strip of cloth had been sewn across the pocket. The young Tonkawa had no idea how much the vest would cost, but he made himself promise to return in a day or so to that store.

As Crooked Path stepped across an alleyway onto the porch of the next store down this main street, the swinging doors flung wide open so suddenly that the edge of one door struck him on his shoulder. Losing his balance momentarily, he reached for the hitching post to his left to prevent a fall into the street. Regaining his balance in an instant, he reached for the knife in his leather scabbard to make sure it had not fallen out.

"Git your hand off that knife, Injun," a deep, angry voice warned.

Crooked Path looked up. Standing in the doorway, a big burly man frowned in his direction. The man's right hand rested on the butt of a pistol in his holster. The Indian boy stood up and straightened his shoulders, his hand still on his knife. He looked into the man's eyes, watching for any movement that would signal trouble, something Crooked Path did not want.

"You hear me, boy?" the menacing voice almost whispered. "Git outta my way or I'll teach you a lesson you ain't ever gonna forget."

Crooked Path held his ground, never taking his eyes off the man's face. The man blinked, then curled his mouth into an evil grin.

"All right, boy," the man said as he stepped toward Crooked Path. He reached for the boy with his giant hand, aiming for a swipe at his throat. As he took a second, long stride from the doorway, the man seemed to lunge at Crooked Path. But the Indian boy no longer stood in that spot. Moving quickly to his left, the Tonkawa let the man's own weight carry his body right on past and onto the horizontal post. The hitching post caught the falling man in his stomach. The man grabbed into the air for help, but his feet left the ground and he flipped over the post, landing on his face in the dusty street.

The man lay in the street for a moment, the air knocked out of him when he hit the ground. He rose to his hands and knees, spit dirt out of his mouth, and turned to look for another assault against the Indian.

But Crooked Path had disappeared, slipping into the shadows of the alley and heading for the back street behind the building. He did not run, but walked quietly and purposefully back across the town to the small camp where his family had set up their *tipi.* He would tell his father what had happened.

The caravan from Woods Prairie rode into Nacogdoches late in the evening of the fifth day of their journey. They came in from the west on the Camino Real which became the main street of the town. Zadock led the four wagons through the town and onto the eastern edge of the community. On previous trips, he had discovered a small grove of pine trees there that made for a suitable campsite. No other travelers had claimed this site yet, and Zadock motioned for the others to select a spot for their wagons and the lean-to tents that would be their home for the next several days. Zadock and Norman marked an area where a campfire would soon be built. Henry and Tonio took the heavy rope from one of the wagons and rigged a small corral among the trees, downwind from the campsite.

After a few minutes of hard work in near darkness, Henry noticed that he was by himself: Tonio was nowhere to be found. Old Wash had gone with Henry's father to arrange for the wagon horses to be reshoed. The Calderons and the Gonzalezes toiled at the campsite. Henry stomped his foot in frustration, knowing exactly where his companion had gone, and returned to his task of finishing the rope corral.

Two hundred yards away, Tonio and Marisol walked hand in hand down the main street of Nacogdoches, peering in the windows of the stores as they passed by. Kerosene lamps lit the small stores that stayed open well into the night during fair days. The two teenagers didn't say very much as they strolled along, preferring to enjoy the silence of just being together, away from their families. Every few steps they would stare into each other's eyes, a shy grin on their faces.

As the couple crossed over to the other side of the wide dirt street, Marisol looked down the block and pointed.

"Tonio, look there," she said, "in that building. Upstairs." He followed her extended arm until he saw the gray shape of a large building standing off to itself. The two-story structure reminded him of Henry's fort-house. As they drew closer, he could see the thick, wide door and a chain across its front. The lower windows were covered with leather flaps, and several portals had been carved out of the walls. When Indians or another enemy attacked, rifles would be poked through these small openings to fire on them. The downstairs of the building was enveloped in darkness. Above, a balcony stretched across the front, with four windows and a doorway opening onto it. An attached barn stood behind the main building. It too was dark.

Now Tonio saw what Marisol had pointed to. A dim light moved from one upstairs window to another. A thin silhouette could barely be seen, like a shadow drifting across an inside room.

"There's someone inside," Marisol said in a whisper. She moved closer to Tonio, resting her right hand on his shoulder.

"I see them," Tonio replied quietly. "It's just someone who lives in this old place, that's all."

"But it looks all locked up," the girl argued. "Maybe it's a thief."

"No," Tonio chuckled at his girlfriend's imagination. "None of our business, that's what it is," he said. "Come on, let's get back to camp." He grasped her hand tightly and led her away from the large building. Ten paces back toward the main street, both of them looked back once more. The upstairs of the house now lay completely dark. Whoever that was upstairs, Tonio thought to himself, either left or turned out the lamp for the night.

No matter, he thought as he walked Marisol back up the street.

CHAPTER SIX

On the following morning, just at first light, Henry awoke to the sounds of wagons rolling by. He looked up from the blanket that lay on the soft pine-needle floor beneath the tall stand of trees. Through the spokes of his own wagon ten yards away he could see the movement of a long wagon drawn by four wide-shouldered oxen. The wagon plodded slowly into the town street. Henry could hear the soft voice of the Mexican driver as he whistled instructions to the reddish-brown beasts who pulled him along. A few paces behind, a smaller ox cartwheeled into sight, a single animal dragging against the rig of the square wooden wagon. It had no driver, but the ox knew to follow close on the heels of the bigger wagon ahead of it. The gray beast shuffled along with its head down, never looking left or right.

Henry came to his feet, tightened his belt, and pulled his floppy cowboy hat onto his head. The wagons reminded him that he had a chore to finish before breakfast. His father had asked him the night before to walk over to the livery and buy a new bit for one of the horses. Henry felt for the coin in his pants pocket: it hadn't fallen out during the night.

I think I'll take someone with me, Henry thought to himself, a sly grin appearing on his face. Tonio hadn't come back from his stroll with Marisol last night until long after Henry had finished tying down the makeshift corral. This called for an early rising, Henry decided. He stepped quietly across the campsite, steering around the embers of the night's fire, and over to the Gonzalez wagon. Just beyond the small tent tied off against their wagon a brightly-colored Mexican blanket draped the ground under a tree. Something lumpy and still lay underneath: Antonio! Henry bent his knees and crept over to the place where his friend lay fast asleep. He gathered up a handful of the soft pine needles on the ground, knelt down beside the blanket, and reached to grab the blanket away. As he did, Tonio blinked his eyes in confusion, still half-asleep. Henry dumped the pine needles right at his friend's chin. Tonio opened his mouth just a fraction, and the dirt and pine cascaded in.

"*Auuggh! Phthew!*" Tonio gagged and spit as he sat upright, now wide awake. "Who's doing that?" he asked as he grabbed the dirt from his mouth. Henry had stood up and stepped back after tossing the pine needles at his friend. Now he began to laugh, his arms around his waist as he bent over in glee.

Tonio threw his blanket at Henry and followed right behind as he lunged off the ground. Tackling his giggling friend just above his knees, Tonio rolled Henry over onto the ground. They wrestled for a moment until Tonio had pinned Henry on his back.

"I'll get you for this," Tonio threatened with a big smile on his face.

"Sshh," Henry said in between chuckles. "You'll wake everyone up."

Tonio looked around. No one stirred at the campsite. He looked back at Henry pinned underneath him. "I will get you," he promised again, and rolled off and up onto his feet. He wiped the back of his arm across his face and spit out one last bit of dirt.

"C'mon," Henry said as he stood up and brushed himself off. "I have to go into town, and you're coming with me."

"Why do I have to go?" Tonio whined. "I can sleep another hour if I want to. You go to town on your own."

"Uh uh," Henry shook his head and wagged his finger. "I had to do the corral all by myself last night while you and Marisol wandered all over the place. You owe me one." As he spoke, Henry began to mimic Tonio walking with his girlfriend, stumbling about with a funny look on his face. "Ohhh Marisol," Henry swooned. "You're so pretty, Marisol. Let me hold your hand, Marisol. Let's go for a walk in the moonlight, Marisol." Henry closed his eyes as he pretended to be his lovestruck friend, and bumped right into Marisol who had been awakened by the voices.

"I wouldn't walk two steps with you, Henry Woods," she said in her most serious voice as she glared at him. "You're not funny." She wrapped a large sleeping blanket around her shoulders with a flare and turned her back on him. "Hmmph," she punctuated her anger by slumping her shoulders.

Henry seemed unconcerned. He smiled at Tonio, who was not amused.

"*Amigo,*" Tonio warned, "we'd better be going or someone standing here is going to be in big trouble." He paused to look in Marisol's direction, but she kept her back turned on both boys. "And it won't be me."

Henry started out from the campsite and headed for town. He took off his hat as he walked, pretending to speak to it as if it were a girl, mumbling Marisol's name as he went. Tonio shook his head and waited one more moment to see if Marisol would speak to him. She didn't budge. Tonio turned and headed after his friend. Some start to this day, he thought to himself as he hurried to catch up with Henry.

In front of the livery stable, the two ox-driven wagons stood unattended while the driver spoke to a tall black man standing in the doorway. As Henry and Tonio approached, they could hear the two men arguing about something. Both were pointing furiously, waving their arms, and talking at the same time, one in a drawling English and the other in a clipped Spanish tone. Neither seemed to understand the other. Above the two men hung a sign, worn and wrinkled from time. It read:

BLACKSMITH and Stables

William Goyens, Prop.

The two boys stopped to watch the odd scene for a moment, not wanting to interrupt such a curious debate. Finally, the cart driver threw up his hands in disgust, issued one last statement in the general direction of the stable owner, and walked back to his large wagon. He poked about at the rigging while the boys walked past him.

"Morning," Henry tipped his hat as he greeted the liveryman.

"'N' to you, sir," William Goyens replied politely. "Out mighty early?"

"Need to buy a bit for my horse, please," Henry responded, fingering the coin in his pocket. His father had said it would be enough.

"Be glad to help you," the man said after a pause. "Come inside and pick one out off my wall." He turned and went inside the dark stable. The boys followed just behind, stopping for a moment to let their eyes adjust to the shadowy room.

Inside the large smith shop the walls were covered with every kind of rig equipment and tool that could be bought this side of the Mississippi River. Because Nacogdoches stood on the main crossroads out of Louisiana and into the rest of Texas, travelers and traders passed through in great numbers year-round. Rough roads caused rigs to break down; bolts and rods fell off in river crossings; horses threw their shoes on the dusty trails. The blacksmith had to have the right piece or part for every occasion. He also had to be experienced enough to know how to fix the broken or missing parts on any wagon. Shoeing horses was usually a side job done in the early morning or late evening hours when the breeze cooled the man as he stood over the anvil, shaping and fastening each metal strip made to order for each horse hoof.

Henry and Tonio had been in liveries at Moore's Ferry and in Mina, just west of Woods Prairie. But they had never seen anything like this: thousands of tools and bits and leather straps, hanging on the shadowed walls or stacked on every flat surface in the building. The boys wandered quietly across the big room, kicking up the dirt floor as they shuffled along staring all around them. No breeze had stirred up the air this August morning and the room felt uncomfortably warm with a smell that combined leather and metal and sweat and stable.

"Excuse me," Henry spoke in the direction of the tall black man who still stood in the doorway. "I need a bit, probably Number Four."

"Silvered?" the smithy asked in a quiet, low voice.

"Yessir, if you have one," Henry replied, then immediately was sorry: of course he would have one. He had one of everything.

"Over to your right, sir," the man jutted his jaw as if pointing with it. "On the table below the crosscut saw hangin' there."

"Here, Henry," Tonio spotted the box first. A dozen bits that had once been stacked neatly now looked like hard silver creatures trying to climb out of their confined space. One bit lay on the table a few inches away from the others, like the lead creature of the escape. Tonio scooped it up and

48

handed it to his friend, who looked it over carefully, feeling its size and weight in his experienced hand.

"This one'll do fine," Henry decided after a moment's study. He reached with his empty hand into his pocket and drew out the coin. Holding it between thumb and pointing finger, he raised it toward the man in the doorway. "Will this be enough?"

The blacksmith walked casually across the room to meet Henry. He took the coin and held it above his head where it caught a glint of light coming through a crack in the far wall.

"Just right, sir. And I thank ye kindly, too." The black man seemed to bow slightly at the waist. His huge shoulders and forearms rippled hard-earned muscles as he bent over. Henry smiled in return, thinking to himself distantly: I sure wouldn't want to wrestle this giant.

"We'll be going back to camp now," Henry said as a farewell. "Thanks again." He and Tonio headed for the doorway as the man watched them leave. As Henry crossed out onto the porch, Tonio stopped as if remembering something, and turned back to look into the livery room.

"Excuse me," Tonio said, "but could you tell me who lives in that big fort up the street?"

William Goyens frowned. "The stone fort? Why, no one. It's been locked up tight for months, ever since the townfolk ran Mr. Peter Bean off."

"Couldn't be locked, though," Tonio responded to the man's statement. "We saw someone in there last night, wandering around upstairs."

"Don't think so," the liveryman insisted. "Walked by there this morning, like every day. Chained and locked just so, ever since winter."

"C'mon, Tonio," Henry interrupted, having stepped back in to catch the conversation. "You and Marisol are just crazy, that's all. Seeing things." He paused and grinned, then looked mockingly serious. "Either that or you both saw a ghost."

The blacksmith gasped out loud as he caught his breath.

"Enough of that talk, boys," he said sternly. "Don't go talking about no ghosts now, you hear? Get along with you now. Be seeing you." Goyens turned and walked back into the dark corner of the big workroom. Tonio shrugged his shoulders and turned with Henry to step outside into the morning light.

"Sure got spooked, didn't he?" Tonio said as he walked past Henry.

"Ghosts," Henry wrinkled his nose. "Hmmph."

CHAPTER SEVEN

A dark figure stood in the creeping shadows of the alleyway alongside the old stone fort. He gazed out into the busy street watching the townspeople walk from store to store. Some paused to look in the shop windows and every once in a while one or two of them would step inside for a closer look. Others moved along briskly, headed for a destination at the other end of town. Because the county fair was in full swing now, the street was crowded most of the day and into the early evening hours. Wagons and carts wheeled noisily through the dirt kicking up dust and scattering a flock of ruddy chickens that pecked at stray seed near the general store porch. Horses of every size and hue carried their riders back and forth through Nacogdoches, creating a sea of movement that ebbed and flowed until the cool breeze signaled a calm for the night.

But hardly anyone came near the old abandoned fort. It stood at one end of the town, just off the main street, locked and boarded up. The warehouse just behind it also stood undisturbed by the crowds, empty except for rats and spiders and copperheads. Leather covers spread across the upstairs portals that had been used years before by sharpshooters during Indian attacks. Chains and thick hemp crisscrossed the front and back doors of the stone fort and the warehouse, and a hand-scribbled sign that read "Closed" still hung by a single nail on one of the doors.

The shadowy figure did not move, except for his eyes which darted from face to face in the crowds that moved across the street from where he hid. He felt safe in this alley next to the fort, a perfect position for spying. No one had any business coming near his watch post, and if they did he could easily disappear behind the building.

Only those two kids had been a nuisance the night before. Foolish, he thought to himself, to be moving inside the fort before midnight. He had spotted the boy and girl as they strolled hand in hand up to the fort, dousing his lamp just a moment too late, just as the girl pointed in his direction. But they had soon walked away, apparently not interested in what they had seen. Still, he reminded himself, he must be more careful. He and the others dared not be caught now, not at this moment.

They were so close to accomplishing their mission. Only two more were unaccounted for, and they should be riding into town today or the next day at the latest. Together they would finish months of planning and preparation. Finally, these arrogant Americans who had come to Mexico would be stopped, and their leaders silenced. Tejas and Coahuila would once again be firmly in the hands of the Mexican government.

Now was no time to be sloppy. If those children showed up again, or anyone else for that matter, they would simply have to "disappear." The Indians would take them as slaves, perhaps, or maybe the river would be the best solution: a watery grave for those who came too close to discovering our plan.

The dark figure smiled to himself. With one last glance out into the streets, he turned and was gone, vanishing in the deep shadows.

CHAPTER EIGHT

Crooked Path stepped onto the porch of the store where the vest still hung in the window. He had been more cautious this trip into the town, deliberately avoiding the saloon where the big white man had tried to attack him. Not wanting to cause any trouble, the Tonkawa had heeded his father's careful instructions. "Walk as the coyote on the hill," he had said. "Everyone can see you but no one will notice you. Every step has a purpose, waste no movement, know that there are enemies behind the rocks."

Crooked Path tightened his grip on the small bundle in his left hand. His mother had wrapped it carefully for him, promising that it would be a good trade for the vest he had seen the day before. He hoped so. Seeing the vest buoyed his spirit: surely it would soon be his. The door to the shop stood open to catch any of the late morning breeze, and he stepped inside, pausing for a moment to let his eyes adjust to the darker atmosphere.

Several white people stood inside the small store, but none glanced his way as he moved toward the counter. Crooked Path did not feel any fear, only some discomfort at being inside the building instead of out in the fresh air and open spaces. He didn't much care for the white man's towns at all, really, although he had only been through a few of them. He waited quietly at the counter until the clerk spotted him, turning away from a small table she was polishing with a yellowed rag. The clerk, a young white woman in a plain blue dress and white apron, smiled in his direction as she stepped to her side of the counter.

"Good day," she said in a pleasant voice. "May I help you?"

Crooked Path nodded and pointed to the window. "I like the vest there." As he spoke he placed the bundle on the counter in front of him. Carefully unwrapping it until the deer hide cover lay flat, he picked up the object he had been carrying and offered it to the young woman. Her eyes widened as she gently held it in both hands.

"Oh, it's beautiful," she said almost in a whisper. She turned the small leather purse over and over in her hands.

Tiny pieces of turquoise and quartz, sewn into the purse, caught and reflected small rays of sunlight inside the store. The drawstring made of deer tendon was tied off in a neat bow that Crooked Path's mother had finished for him.

"For the vest?" the Tonkawa asked hopefully. The clerk looked into his deep brown eyes for a moment as she smiled.

"I think this would be a grand trade," she nodded as she turned toward the window display. With the small purse still in her hand, she reached for the vest on its wooden hangar.

"I'll be takin' that vest, Injun," a strange, low voice suddenly interrupted the tranquil store. Oh no, thought Crooked Path, trouble: it must be that big ugly man who came after me yesterday. He stood with his back to the door, both hands on the counter, ready in an instant to turn to the danger.

"You hear me, boy?" the odd voice boomed again. "Get away from that counter and look at me when I talk to you."

Crooked Path squinted in concentration, bent his knees slightly to prepare to move quickly, and dropped his right hand from the counter and to his side, inches away from the knife in his belt. He inhaled a small breath in anticipation and turned to face the man.

"I thought that was you!" the voice sang out once more. Crooked Path's eyes nearly popped out of their sockets.

"Henry Woods?!"

"How in the world did you end up in Nacogdoches?" Henry asked his Tonkawa friend in amazement.

"My father brought many families from our village to trade here," Crooked Path explained in his simple fashion. "Look," he continued, "I am trading for that vest." He pointed to the window display.

"And let me get that for you," the clerk interrupted as she leaned over the countertop and took the vest off of its hangar. She began to fold the vest on a sheet of grey cloth that would serve as wrapping, but Crooked Path stopped her.

"I would like to wear it," he said. The clerk smiled and nodded. "Of course," she said. Crooked Path took the vest gently in his hands, admiring its stitching and colors up close for the first time. He swung it around his neck and stuck his arms through the side openings. The vest fit as if it had been made for him by his own mother. He squared his shoulders in an uncharacteristic show of pride as Henry watched with amusement.

"Good-looking vest," Henry said. "Come with me to our camp. My family is here, and Tonio. I know they want to see you."

"I cannot go now," Crooked Path answered as the two friends walked outside into the dusty midday heat. "My father wants me to return quickly because of what happened." Henry raised his eyebrows at that, and Crooked Path briefly told him of the encounter the day before. "When you spoke in that strange voice," he concluded, "I thought it was the ugly white man again."

Henry chuckled. "Remind me to be more careful behind your back," he said jokingly. "I will come find you tonight, Crooked Path. Can you meet me at the old stone fort at the end of town?"

"I know this fort," the Tonkawa nodded as he turned to go. "I will meet you there after the sun has gone."

Chapter 8

"See you then," Henry waved as he walked east through town. What a strange coincidence, he thought to himself as he headed for camp. And what a great surprise to see my friend here.

CHAPTER NINE

"As for me, my fellow Texans, if this means **war**, then so be it! Let there be a great revolution in this country, not unlike the one our fathers struck for liberty and for a new nation on this earth! May God bless us in our efforts for freedom from tyranny forever!"

The small audience erupted in applause and cheers, with several men bellowing out "Huzzahs!" above the noise of the crowd. Thomas Rusk beamed with defiance and delight at the crowd's response to his speech, bending slightly at the waist in a bow to the cheers. He stepped down from the tree stump where he had stood to speak and shook hands with the first few men who greeted him.

"What about Wharton?" hollered a voice in the middle of the crowd.

"He's with us," Rusk shouted back. "When he spoke in Columbia last week, he called for the raising of a Texas militia to show Santa Anna we mean business."

"What about Colonel Austin?" another voice shouted above the din.

This brought the crowd to silence. Rusk paused for a moment and frowned.

"We haven't heard from Esteban yet," he replied, carefully choosing his words. "We know he is on his way back from Mexico City, and may be in New Orleans by now. But no one has spoken to him since Santa Anna released him from prison." Rusk paused again. "Surely two years in a Mexican jail will turn any man, even the Colonel. We need him with us, but we'll fight without his blessing if it comes to that!" Rusk's voice raised to a shout at the end of his statement, bringing the crowd to a loud cheer all over again.

Henry and Tonio stood at the edge of the crowd, astounded at the scene they were witnessing. Their fathers had accompanied Señor Calderon to the hastily called meeting at the east end of town and the boys had tagged along out of curiosity. Marisol's father had explained on the way that he had met Thomas and Polly Rusk the year before when the Rusks had come to Texas from Georgia. Rusk, he told them, had chased some land speculators across the country after they had stolen investments from him, and ended up in east Texas. When he discovered the beautiful open forest lands of this region, he brought his family here to live.

"He is a good, honest man," Calderon explained. "But I am concerned about his opinions against our government. He will cause trouble in Texas, I am afraid."

The boys and the rest of the crowd, about twenty-five men who had gathered, had heard Rusk talk about the meeting he had just attended on the Brazos, where he and other Texans had called for the organization of what they named a war party to defy the restrictions of General Santa Anna, dictator of Mexico. Rusk explained what most of the men already knew, that Santa Anna had taken too much control of their lives, and that it would only get worse. The borders into the United States were being closed again, and the harbors on the coast were being patrolled, again, by customs officials and Mexican soldiers.

Henry's mind reeled with the talk of revolution. He imagined himself as a soldier in a vast army crossing Texas and fighting the Mexicans under Santa Anna. Cannons boomed in his imagination, and flags waved. At one point during Rusk's speech, Tonio punched his friend in the ribs to get his attention, spoiling the exciting daydream.

Zadock Woods turned out of the crowd and headed up the street. Henry followed several steps before another voice sounded above the murmuring crowd.

"What about Sam?" the voice shouted. "What does Houston say?"

Everyone stopped, including Henry and his father. Rusk looked over the crowd and smiled as he caught the eye of a tall, broad-shouldered man

in the middle of the throng. The man cleared his throat dramatically.

"Perhaps Mr. Houston should speak for himself, seeing as how he's standing right next to you," Sam Houston said in a clear, distinctive voice.

Several men laughed. Then everyone became very still. The famous Tennessee congressman was known all across the frontier, and his opinion was highly respected by most.

"I appreciate Mr. Rusk's forthright opinion on the subject of war," Houston began in a casual Tennessee drawl, "although I would counsel a great deal of thought as to such a plan of action. I am not against a fight for freedom - well, to be honest with you boys, I haven't ever turned away from any fight against anything!" The crowd chuckled at this: Ole Sam had a reputation for "rasslin" that even included a knockdown bout with a fellow congressman back in Washington, D.C.

"But we can't go half-cocked into a duel with General Santa Anna. He's got an army that's followed him from one end of Mexico to the other, and they're mighty loyal to him. He's got 'em fighting down in Zacatecas right now, and I wouldn't bet my good horse against him." The crowd murmured in agreement. "If we rile him, he'll come after us. And he won't stop until the matter's taken care of, one way or the other."

"Let him come!" someone yelled from the crowd. That started another round of cheers and noise. Henry grinned at Tonio. This was fun listening to men like Sam Houston.

"Well," Houston quieted the crowd by motioning with his long arms, "if he does come up here to shut us down," he paused for effect, "I hope you boys will join me: we'll meet him at the Rio Grande!"

With this the crowd burst into a long series of shouts and hurrahs, men slapping each other on the back while others raised a rifle or pistol high in the air. Henry got caught up in the festive spirit, hollering and clapping with the others. His father also joined in: Zadock had fought too many enemies along the frontier to be stopped now by a Mexican dictator.

Sam Houston let the clamor continue for a minute or more before silencing the audience for one last statement.

"Now friends," he concluded, "let me suggest only this: listen to what Stephen Austin will say. He deserves our attention for all he's done for Texas. And he is a wise man. Mr. Rusk, I agree with you. I have a notion that prison has changed Mr. Austin's thinking. When he comes over from New Orleans, let's hear him out." Houston looked around the crowd. "As for me, my talking has parched my throat and plum deafened me." The crowd laughed. "I'm headed for the saloon, and hope y'all will join me." The men shouted one more cheer as the tall Tennessean moved down the street with his typically long strides. About a dozen men filed after him while the others began to disperse. Zadock motioned to Henry to follow him back to the campsite, and the boys joined Mr. Calderon and Mr. Gonzalez as they headed up the street.

"War, Tonio," Henry said excitedly. "What do you think? Do you think we'll fight Santa Anna? When do you suppose he'll come to Texas?"

Tonio waved his hand in Henry's face to quiet him down. "Don't know what's going to happen, *compadre*," he replied. "I do know one thing, though. If General Santa Anna comes to Texas, he won't be coming alone. There'll be the whole Mexican army marching right behind him. It'll be a sight, that's for sure."

CHAPTER TEN

The sun lowered past the tops of the tall evergreens that crowded the western hills outside of Nacogdoches. It seemed to grow suddenly much larger than it had been higher in the sky, and its yellow hue blended into an orange, then crimson ball of fire. The sky joined in on the prism pattern, darkening to several shades of blue. And wispy clouds reflected all of the sunset colors as if a painter's brush had skipped across the evening sky. If anyone had been watching, they would have seen a pinpoint of white appear on the western horizon, peeking just through the treetops. It grew brighter as the colors surrounding it faded to black.

"There," Marisol pointed. "' Evening star, very far. Grant me this, just one wish.'" She closed her eyes tight for a few seconds and gripped Tonio's hand tighter at the same moment. Tonio stared at her, amused. When she opened her eyes again, she turned to him. "Did you make a wish?"

"Well, uh, I -" he started.

"Don't tell me," she interrupted stammering. "If you tell someone your wish it won't come true, you know." Tonio nodded warily as if he knew this to be a fact. "I made a wish, a wonderful wish," she continued. "I wish I could tell you." She giggled at her little play on words. Tonio smiled, still a little uncertain how he was supposed to respond. If he had made a wish, it would have been only to be right where he was, doing exactly what he was doing: walking hand in hand, alone, with Marisol. He couldn't imagine anything any better at the moment.

"Do you want to keep walking this way?" he asked timidly. "We're pretty far out of town." He glanced back over his shoulder. The town still shone brightly with candle lamps and campfires even though most of the people had retired for the evening, back to their homes or wagons, or into the saloons. The little path they had followed, no more than a deer trail, had wandered off the main road and to the edge of the forest. They had walked about a half-mile, strolling slowly, saying very little. Occasionally their eyes would meet for an instant and both teenagers would smile and then shyly look away.

"Let's stop for a minute, Antonio," Marisol answered. "I want to watch the stars come out."

"There's a tree down over there," he pointed through the darkness. Leading her by the hand, Tonio strode to the huge log that had once been a great fir tree standing proudly at the edge of the forest. It had supplied shade and nesting limbs for generations of creatures. Now it would be a good place for two young people to sit and have an undisturbed moment together. Tonio brushed across the log with his shirt sleeve to clean off any cobwebs or dirt, and then gently lifted Marisol up onto the fallen tree. With an easy hop, he joined her, taking her hand back into his.

They sat for several minutes without saying a word. Marisol stared up into the night sky, and Tonio glanced about watching the forest move ever so slightly in its special way. The forest, like the flat plains where he lived, created its own motion and was never completely still. Sometimes the wind made the grass and trees dance. Sometimes the animals lent a hand. And sometimes it seemed as if the land had its own spirit, a personality that breathed and sang -

Tonio shook his head. I don't know what I'm thinking, he said to himself. I'm just glad I'm here.

As if she had read his mind, Marisol chose that very instant to lean over and lay her head on Tonio's shoulder. She closed her eyes and smiled.

"It's so nice out here, Antonio," she whispered. "All the beautiful stars." Tonio reached his arm around her waist. Marisol snuggled a little harder against him.

Tonio gulped. "You're, uhm, Marisol, you sure are...I mean -" he gulped a second time, "You're a whole lot more beautiful than the stars," he finally managed to blurt out. His own words made him freeze for an instant, wondering if he had said the right thing.

"Oh, Tonio," Marisol sighed, "what a lovely thing to say." She turned her head up from his shoulder and kissed him just between his chin and cheek. He squeezed her waist a little tighter and exhaled the breath he had been holding far too long. Whew, he thought to himself.

A twig snapped loudly behind them. Its sudden sound seemed much louder because of the silence of the moment. Tonio sat up straight and turned, causing Marisol to lift her head up. A second twig popped and then Tonio could hear the very distinctive sound of footsteps in the woods not twenty paces away. He looked right into Marisol's large brown eyes and brought his finger to his lips. "SShhh," he motioned without making the noise. She nodded silently, knowing this was a moment for caution.

Tonio slid off the log and helped Marisol down to the ground next to him. Taking her hand again, he crept along the length of the fallen tree until he could make his way around the huge spider web of roots that towered in the air in front of him. The two teenagers paid close attention to each step they took, careful to avoid any branch, walking along the carpet of tree needles that blanketed the ground.

The footsteps they had heard continued just ahead of them, moving slowly. Tonio sensed that there might be several people in the secretive group that made its way through the night forest. His curiosity got the best of him now: he had to find out who these people were and why they would be moving deeper into the shadowy woods.

Tonio and Marisol paused next to a thicket of underbrush, leaning against the trunk of a tall cedar. They held their breaths and listened.

The footsteps were silent. The group had stopped only a few paces along the trail. Tonio squinted to see any movement but the darkness enveloped everything except vague shades of gray - the trees.

A different sound penetrated the forest solitude. Marisol leaned up to Tonio's ear and whispered, "Voices." Tonio turned his head to listen. At first, the sound was garbled and soft; gradually, the two tuned in to the quiet sounds and could pick out the conversation that had commenced.

"Flores, you must not be seen in the town," the loudest, clearest voice said. "This is imperative. Do you understand?"

"*Si,* I understand," a second, lower voice replied.

"*Bueno,*" the first voice said. "If *El Commandante* discovers that you have been this far north, we will both have to answer to him. Our orders are very clear, *no?*"

"Yes, I know, *Capitan,*" the second person answered quickly. "But what of the Cherokees? Have you spoken with Chief Bowles?"

"Not yet," came the reply. "I have sent two agents to the Upper Brazos only yesterday. They will return with his answer by the end of the week."

"Very well. What shall I do as long as I am here?"

"I have two messages that must be sent to Bexar as soon as possible. One is a report that must reach *El Presidente* without delay. The other is the list of those who are to be arrested. I will know by the day after tomorrow where each of the traitors will be on the first of September. Will you deliver these for us?" the stronger voice asked.

"Of course," said the other. "I will meet you at the appointed location in two nights."

"Bueno. Hasta luego," the first voice concluded.

There was a shuffling of feet as the men parted company in the dark forest. Tonio and Marisol knelt down by the thicket and froze in place. Two shadows walked right past them, not an arm's reach away. Two other pairs of feet stumbled in another direction, popping twigs every few paces. The two motionless teens waited for what seemed like forever but was only three minutes before they stood. They listened for another whole minute before speaking.

"Antonio, what was that all about?" Marisol spoke first.

"I don't know," he said. "Someone is in a lot of trouble, it sounds like."

"People are to be arrested," she remarked, remembering what the voices had said. "Do you suppose they were speaking of criminals?"

"' Traitors,'" Tonio repeated. "But why would anyone come to this place in the middle of the night to speak about traitors?" He paused. "No, I don't get it."

"Tonio, take me home." Marisol tried not to sound afraid but she no longer felt comfortable away from the town.

"All right," he said. "We'll be all right now." He tried to sound reassuring but felt uneasy himself.

Hand in hand they walked quickly but carefully out of the forest, past the log where they had sat only minutes earlier, unaware of trouble coming so very near them that night.

But trouble was not finished with them yet.

CHAPTER ELEVEN

The word spread quickly through Nacogdoches during the morning hours: General Cos had been reported moving out of Mexico and toward Texas with a portion of the regular army! Many people believed it to be nothing more than a rumor. There had been trouble in this northernmost province all summer long, but no one really believed it serious enough to call for the Mexican troops again. The incident at Anahuac in June had been an odd repeat of an earlier crisis in 1832, but everyone had calmed down since.

Questions ran through the crowds like a prairie fire. Would President Santa Anna actually send General Cos, his brother-in-law, up to Texas? What about the rebellion still going on south of Mexico City? What about Stephen F. Austin and his imminent return to Texas? Would the self-proclaimed "Texas War Party" of William Wharton send out an alarm? Was a revolution brewing these hot summer days of 1835?

One person might have the answers to these questions. One person in Nacogdoches might know whether this frightening information was fact or rumor. That person was Vicente Cordova. Cordova had served in the Mexican government for years and knew the leaders in Mexico City, Saltillo, and San Antonio de Bexar very well. He understood the politics of his day and, perhaps most importantly, understood how men like General Cos, General Filisola, and President Antonio Lopez de Santa Anna thought.

Cordova was a popular personality often seen in Texas. Congenial and fluent in several languages, he could be found along the Texas trade routes speaking with merchants, welcoming new citizens, and generally extending a friendly spirit to those around him. An intelligent man and excellent speaker, Cordova was called on many times to clarify situations on the frontier just like this.

Henry Woods had heard his father speak of Cordova before and now listened intently as Zadock considered the present rumors flying with Manuel Gonzalez and Jesus

Calderon. This seemed to Henry an exciting time, what with rumors about rebellion, marching armies, and so on. The trip to Nacogdoches had been far more entertaining already than just attending an annual fair.

"I spoke with Mr. Rusk after breakfast," Zadock Woods concluded his conversation at the campsite, "and he said that Cordova would speak at the town square at Noon. If there's to be a war, I'll fight for the freedom that we've earned here in Texas. But I'll fight at home, not here two hundred miles away." The other men nodded vigorously in agreement. Freedom in Texas had been severely restricted since the decree of 1830, and despite the protests of men like Austin and Travis, and now Houston, Santa Anna continued to urge the Mexican Congress to apply pressure to the Northern provinces.

But when the fighting began, if there was to be any at all, every man and woman on the frontier preferred to do battle in their own backyard, defending their homes and families and everything they had toiled for over the years.

"If Cos is coming this way," Mr. Calderon chimed in, "I'll meet him at Mina with my neighbors at my side."

Zadock smiled in silent agreement. "Señor Woods, should we make plans to return to our homes?"

"Not yet," Zadock replied after a moment's hesitation. "Let's hear Cordova out first, and then we can decide. If Cos is marching north, we can be home days ahead of his army if need be."

As the men stood and walked to their own wagons, Henry looked around for Tonio. He hadn't seen him all morning. And Tonio and Marisol must have come in late the night before after Henry had fallen asleep. He must find his friend now, he thought. This was the kind of news that signaled adventure! He sprinted to the area where Tonio usually slept but found his bedroll already tied off and leaning against a nearby barrel.

Frustrated, Henry left the campsite and headed into town. The summer sun already baked the dusty street and a midmorning breeze blew only hot wind down the path he walked. Perspiration beaded on his forehead and trickled down the back of his neck. Ignoring the heat, he glanced in every store and down each alley looking for his Tejano friend. But no Tonio appeared.

Henry reached the west end of the main street of town without recognizing anyone in the street crowds. He turned to face where he'd just walked, with his hands jammed on his hips in disgust. "Tonio, where are you?" he said quietly but firmly to himself.

Just then he noticed out of the corner of his eye the swishing skirts of several women coming out of a small dress shop to his right. He looked absently in their direction, then did a double-take as he recognized his mother in the lead.

"Mother!" he called out as he started toward her. She looked up, as did Mrs. Calderon, Mrs. Gonzalez, and Marisol, who trailed behind the others. They all grinned at him in unison, and Marisol waved then frowned at him as she remembered she was still supposed to be mad at him from the day before. Henry caught up to them quickly and let Minerva Woods lean over and peck his cheek with a motherly kiss.

"Henry, you looked upset about something a moment ago," she said in a questioning tone. "Is something the matter?"

"No, Mother," he replied. "I'm just looking for Antonio, and I can't find him anywhere." At that, Marisol looked up, her eyes squinting in concern.

Henry turned to her. "Have you seen him this morning?"

"Yes, but just for a moment after breakfast," Marisol answered, thinking as she spoke slowly. "He told me he was -" She stopped and glanced furtively at the three mothers who stood there listening idly to the conversation. "Henry, will you walk with me over to the apple seller? Mother, Henry will see me back to camp." She reached up and kissed her mother, took Henry by his elbow, and pushed him away from the others. Henry gave her a curious look but went with her: she had a tight hold on his arm that signaled urgency.

The three women watched with light surprise as the two teens hurried away. They shook their heads as if to say, We don't understand these children and resumed their stroll down the crowded street.

"Marisol, what got into you?" Henry asked in mock surprise.

"Henry Woods, you listen to me and don't interrupt," she said.

"What do you mean -" he began, but she pinched his elbow harder, and he shut up.

"I'm worried about Antonio," she began. "After breakfast, he told me he was going to the forest and then go looking for you. I thought he was with you all this time, and now you come along and say you haven't seen him this morning? At all?" Henry shook his head, confused. "I'm frightened for him-"

"What are you talking about?" Henry interrupted anyway. "What forest? Why was he going into the forest?"

"We went there last night," Marisol replied, and then quickly told Henry about the strange voices in the dark woods. When she had finished, Henry looked out past the edge of town, past the old stone fort that stood alone, and along the main road that wound into the dense forest.

"C'mon," Henry took her hand and pulled. "Show me where you were last night."

Marisol did not need any more persuading. She walked quickly past Henry and headed for the woods, grabbing the layers of her skirt up with both hands so as not to trip as she hurried along. Henry kept up her pace as they left the town buildings behind them and most of the crowds. Marisol led Henry for several minutes along the main road, then darted off across a meadow. After a hundred steps or so along a narrow deer trail, the two passed a huge fallen tree lying on its side and then found themselves in the permanent shadows of the tall evergreens. Marisol did not hesitate but pressed on into the dense forest. Henry's eyes scoured the woods in every direction, his hand still grasping Marisol's. The sun barely penetrated this part of the forest and it seemed a few degrees cooler, although no breeze could make its way here either.

Finally, Marisol stopped, so suddenly that Henry nearly ran into her. They stood as if frozen in place. The creaking sound of a wagon wheel echoed dimly from far away on the main road. A red cardinal thrashed its way through a nearby underbrush. No other noises broke the silence.

"Here," Marisol said simply after a minute's pause. "This is where we heard the voices."

"Tell me again about the voices," Henry insisted, breaking the eerie quiet with his words.

"I told you what we heard, Henry," she replied. "They spoke in whispers. We couldn't understand every word: they mumbled their English."

"What do you mean?" Henry asked, a clue now presented to him.

"Their English was not very good, you know," she repeated. "Their Spanish was much clearer."

"They were Tejanos?" Henry asked.

"I suppose," the girl answered, trying to think back to the voices.

"Or*Mexican*!" Henry spoke with emphasis. "Could they have been Mexican spies?"

"Well, how would we know that?" Marisol sounded insulted.

"Never mind," Henry said, interrupting her. "Help me look around here. Maybe we can find a clue. Tonio may be in big trouble."

At this Marisol's heart beat faster and she blinked several times quickly to keep the tears from streaming down her face. She swallowed hard and looked straight into Henry's eyes. "Is Antonio all right?"

"Of course he is," Henry said, trying to sound reassuring. "And we'll find him soon. He probably has gone on the trail of those men from last night." Henry had a thought. "If he did, he would leave clues for us." And with that, Henry began to move across the small area where they stood, bent over at the waist as he stared at the ground. Marisol followed his example and walked up the needle-carpeted deer trail for several paces. Both teens looked for some sign of their friend for several minutes without speaking. Suddenly Marisol cried out.

"Henry, come here," she said, motioning frantically with one hand. Henry dashed over to her side and looked where she was pointing. "Look at this," she said in a tense whisper. She bent over and picked up a shiny object that had lain against a small tree trunk. "It's a *gallon*," she said.

"From Tonio's belt," Henry began.

"Yes," Marisol interrupted him. "He was wearing his belt this morning. It's the one I made for him for his birthday. What does it mean?"

"He's leaving us a trail," Henry replied simply. "Come on, Marisol," he said grabbing her empty hand as she gripped the shiny silver object in the other. "He went up this way." They both looked deeper into the forest shadows. Marisol squeezed Henry's hand. He smiled his bravest smile and started up the twisting path. Somewhere ahead, they would find Tonio.

CHAPTER TWELVE

The trail meandered through the woods like a long string that had been tossed into the forest. It skirted the small meadows and at one point seemed to dead-end at the banks of a tiny, brackish pond overgrown with water plants and lined with croaking frogs. Henry had walked to the left around the pond where he happened on to the third round *gallon* from Tonio's belt. It lay on the ground where the trail started up again; the trail still moved west and deeper into the thick forest. He waved for Marisol, who had walked to the north around the pond, and she joined him a minute later.

The second silver object had been jammed into the crook of a tree at eye level nearly three hundred yards from the first sign. Henry estimated that they had walked a half-mile at least. He had also noticed that more than one person had come along this trail, and recently. The carpet of evergreen needles had been disturbed by footsteps not only on the trail but beside it as well. Maybe three people had come here, probably since the night before according to the way the brown needles lay broken and piled. One of those was Tonio.

They walked along the rediscovered trail, neither speaking, their eyes cutting in every direction into the shadows that surrounded them. The trail straightened out for nearly two hundred paces, then bent left around thick, thorny underbrush, and resumed its westerly course.

A flash of white startled both teenagers! Marisol gasped and Henry reached for the knife at his belt as they both dropped into a crouch. Henry gritted his teeth in determination, angry at himself for being so surprised by the figure that sprang up just ahead of him. He tensed, the muscles in his legs and shoulders tight, prepared to meet the intruder. He looked through the shadows.

The white-tailed deer leapt a second time, disturbed from its resting place. The doe's tail flagged the white flash again as she disappeared into the woods.

Henry breathed a deep sigh of relief. Marisol shook her head as if to dispel the fear that had gripped her a moment earlier. The forest became eerily still again.

A single shaft of sunlight pierced the darkening woods up ahead, just by chance reflecting its bright ray of the fourth *gallon from* Tonio's belt. The silver piece lay on the stump of an old rotting tree trunk just beside the dwindling trail. Marisol spotted it first and ran ahead of Henry, picking up the tiny object as gently as if it were a whippoorwill egg. She turned the object over in her hands until Henry caught up with her.

"He has four more to leave for us, Henry," she whispered, the silence of the forest affecting her speech. "We have to find him soon."

"We will, Marisol," Henry said confidently. "Look," he pointed ahead, "you can see the edge of a meadow where the trail comes out." She nodded as she spotted the opening. "We'll be able to see way ahead from there." As if to hurry the moment, Marisol struck out onto the trail, her stride long and deliberate. Henry thought to himself, She's determined to find Tonio, that's for sure. He admired her energy: she hadn't fallen behind one time so far during their search.

Henry caught up with the Tejano girl just as they both stepped to the edge of the meadow. The trail disappeared in the knee-high grass that had turned brown in the late summer heat, making the flatland dingy and sad-looking. The black-tipped ears of a jackrabbit stood out above the grass off to Henry's left. He ignored the hare but noted that it stood in alarm: did it see something out there that Henry should know about?

Henry pointed wordlessly to his right, indicating that they should skirt the meadow staying in the shadows of the woods. Marisol nodded that she understood and launched off ahead of him again. Henry shook his head in amazement and grinned as he loped behind.

They had walked nearly halfway around the meadow when Henry heard the noise. He grasped at Marisol's elbow and slid behind a tree at the same time. Confused for an instant, Marisol looked around, then bent to a crouch as she too heard the sound. No bird had whistled, nor any other call by nature. This distinctive noise echoed roughly across the meadow. A creaking wagon wheel, followed by the low voice of someone hollering, broke the quietness.

Then came the snort of a mule, probably angry at being hollered at, and the snapping sound of a driver's whip, popping like a firecracker. Henry could just make out the rumbling of the wagon as it picked up speed moving away from them across the meadow. The sound spurred them both to action as they began to run directly across the open area without thinking of safety for the moment. Henry quickly outdistanced Marisol even though she ran evenly and athletically. Forty paces took them to the middle of the meadow, and then forty more as they approached the far line of trees. They did not listen for the wagon noises as they ran, and the perspiration ran down their necks as they raced along. Without any evidence of the fact, they ran toward a sound that meant finding Tonio.

Henry skidded to a stop as he reached the far edge of the meadow. He could easily make out the ruts of a wagon road heading into the woods and now could hear the creaking wheels again. Marisol soon ran up to his side, grabbing his right arm as she slid to a halt and wiping her brow against his shirt sleeve.

Dust hung in the air along the road, tossed there by the wagon and the two mules that pulled it. Henry could barely make out the rear of the wagon as it moved heavily down the old timber road. But he could make out at least three figures silhouetted atop the rumbling longcart. The back of the driver stood taller than the others as he sat on the high seat in the front, occasionally cracking his whip out over his head and forward onto the back of the black mules. A second figure sat on the side rail of the wagon to the left, gripping the rail to keep his balance and looking ahead past the driver.

The third figure sat on the opened tailgate of the wagon, his legs swinging over the edge. He sat very still in a strange fashion, Henry thought as he stared until he realized two things. First, the figure was tied up, his arms bound tightly against his sides, and what looked like a kerchief around his mouth.

And second...the figure was Antonio!

"Marisol," Henry spoke rapidly and with urgency, "you must get back to town and find your father and mine. I'll follow the wagon."

"But Tonio's -" she began.

"I know, I know," Henry raised his hand to settle her down. "He'll be fine. I can stay up with them. Now listen: you must head north through the woods there." He pointed.

"The main road can't be far. Turn right and get to town. Bring Father here and he can follow the road. Tell him what we saw." Marisol began to protest, but Henry grabbed her by both arms and looked right into her eyes. Without another word, she hugged him quickly and turned away. In an instant, she was running at full speed. Henry watched her until she disappeared into the woods north of the meadow.

Henry took off down the road, being sure to stay off to the far left side so he wouldn't be spotted. Piles of rocks and fallen logs became frustrating obstacles as he ran, but he kept his eyes on the ground to keep from tripping. The wagon continued to plod along and Henry quickly shortened the distance between him and Tonio's kidnappers. After five minutes of running, he forced himself to slow down, not wanting to come too close and be seen. He walked briskly, conserving energy and staying in the shadows whenever he could. Sweat poured down his face and neck, soaking his kerchief and his cotton shirt until they turned black against his chest.

The wagon continued on, the road seldom straying from its westerly route. The wheels squeaked, the whip popped and the mules shuffled along. Henry thought he heard voices once but couldn't be sure. He wanted to rescue his best friend but the risks were too high for the moment. If only he could let him know that help was on the way.

Henry decided he must try to signal Tonio. He stopped for a moment to gather his thoughts and decide on a plan of action. He glanced into the forest on both sides of the lumberjack road. The trees seemed more thinned out on the other side from where he stood: he could make better time there. Taking a deep breath and letting it out slowly as he counted one-two-three, Henry dashed across the road and dove for cover, rolling into the woods as the pine needles pricked his arms and face and stuck to his wet shirt.

He came to his feet in an instant, brushing off the needles as he began to run. He zigzagged through the trees, avoiding the thorn bushes, stumbling once on a boulder that he did not see in the shadows. He made up ground in a hurry, the sounds of the wagon increasing as he neared. Ten more paces, and then another five, and he began to slow down. He could make out the wagon more clearly now as it trudged along not twenty yards ahead of him and to the left.

Chapter 12

There, just ahead, he noted to himself: a brief clearing cut across the path he would take.

Henry slowed to a walk as he came to the narrow *sendera.* He turned abruptly to his left, took five steps to the edge of the road, and looked forward, catching Tonio's widening eyes as the two friends suddenly spotted one another. The figure next to Tonio had disappeared.

CHAPTER THIRTEEN

Marisol ran as fast she could, hiking the folds of her skirt above her knees with both hands. She dashed across the western edge of the brown meadow and into the safety of the shaded woods. With no trail to follow for the moment, she slowed to a brisk walk, having to bend and twist her way for the next hundred paces. She quickly lost any sense of direction but kept walking on what she believed to be the right path. Uncertainty gripped her for a fleeting moment but she shook it away as if it were no more than the cobweb she had just brushed off her face and neck. Focusing on getting back to town - to save Antonio - kept her calm and determined.

She stumbled out onto the main caravan road so suddenly that she nearly walked right across it and into the woods on the other side. It had appeared out of the deep forest without warning. She stopped and took several deep breaths, looking both ways in hopes that a friendly rider or wagon would come along at that moment. But the road remained empty and silent.

Marisol tucked the hem of her skirt into its waistband, folding it up out of the way. Her white *pantalones* reaching down below her knees made her look ridiculous with her skirt bunched up around her hips, but fashion was not her concern at the moment.

With one last glance back to the west, she turned toward Nacogdoches and began to run. Her first strides were quick but exhausting, so she settled instead into an easier pace, pumping her arms evenly and looking straight ahead. She ran along the crest of the old Mexican *real*, never straying off to either side, racing economically and with purpose. Years of swimming and running helped her now in this emergency, and her legs did not give up as she loped in an almost musical rhythm. Perspiration drenched her neck and shoulders, matting her beautiful, long black hair against her shoulders.

Marisol covered the first mile of the road and felt her breathing grow heavier. Tears and beads of sweat glistened around her eyes and cheeks, forcing her to wipe them away every few strides with the back of her hand. She almost tripped once, not seeing a stray tree limb fall across the middle of the road. She caught herself quickly, regained her balance, and ran on.

Ahead she could barely make out the top of a building shimmering like a mirage in the midday heat. The old stone fort! She knew that she could make the last quarter-mile into town: a cry for help would surely bring rescuers to her aid.

Movement to her left made her glance quickly in that direction. Something colorful and not a part of the green and brown forest appeared off to that side. Marisol slowed her pace just enough to get a clearer look: a *tipi* stood in a small clearing and several people sat on the ground just in front of its circular opening. A group of little children ran like quail across the clearing, laughing and hollering in high-pitched tones.

Making an instant decision, Marisol veered to her left directly toward the *tipi* without slowing down, stumbling off the main road and across a small ditch until she reached the soft grass of the clearing. The adults who sat on the ground looked up as she approached, warily but without alarm. The children did not notice her as they ran off. Marisol did not slow until she had nearly bumped into the first woman she came to, finally skidding to a stop and bending over to catch a breath before she spoke. The four people, all women, stared calmly and patiently at the sweat-soaked, disheveled Tejano girl.

"I need your help," Marisol managed to blurt out, her breath still coming in giant heaves and her mouth as dry as cotton balls. She guessed that they would not understand and that she would have to repeat herself, but she glanced up in surprise as two of the women came instantly to their feet. One walked right at her and put her arm around her shoulders, while the other turned toward the clearing and called out in a loud voice. She shouted in her native Tonkawa tongue, beginning and ending her call with a shrill *ree-ree-ree* sound.

The children who had been running screeched to a halt at this warning signal, huddling together immediately and crouching close to the ground. From the edge of the clearing, almost at the same moment that the squaw had finished her shout, three men came running out of the shadows. The first man drew his tomahawk from its sheath even as he picked up speed. The runner just behind him and to his right had his right hand on the knife at his belt. The third runner, shorter and having to pump his legs much faster to keep up -

"Crooked Path!" Marisol screamed as she recognized Antonio's friend coming across the clearing. At the sound of his own name, the Tonkawa boy's brown eyes bulged wide open and he ran right past the two older men and up to Marisol.

A flurry of excitement swept across the clearing as other tribe members appeared out of nowhere, everyone looking for the danger that had been signaled moments before. Marisol stood up as straight as she could, her hands on her hips as she drew in another deep breath.

"It's Tonio," she gasped.

"What has happened?" Crooked Path asked in a quiet but concerned voice. Marisol replied by relating the main events of the previous hours, occasionally having to stop and take in more air to her tired lungs. An Indian woman brought her a hollowed bone cup filled with water which she drank eagerly. Marisol nodded her thanks and finished her story:

Antonio had been kidnapped and Henry was following the trail of the wagon, off to the west, she pointed.

The several adults murmured in their language. Crooked Path frowned as he listened and thought. The woman who had shouted the alarm earlier now waved at the children still huddled together as they had been taught. Immediately they resumed their children's game as if nothing had ever interrupted them.

Crooked Path turned to a third woman and spoke rapidly in the Tonkawa tongue. She nodded and reached for a thin, colorful shawl that lay on the ground, draping it over one shoulder and walking toward Marisol. "Go with my mother," Crooked Path instructed the Tejano girl. "She will walk with you into town where you must find your father and anyone else who will help. You must go quickly."

"But Crooked Path, what about -" she began but he raised one open hand.

"It will be all right," he said calmly and with a forced smile. "I will find our friends. And then you and the others will find me. Now go." And before she could protest he had turned and headed for the main road, swinging to his right and quickly vanishing in the shadows of the trees on the other side.

Crooked Path's mother took Marisol gently by one elbow and began to walk her toward town. She did not speak but moved the two of them quickly along.

Tonio had wished in that instant that he could shout at his friend Henry who had so suddenly appeared out of the forest. But the kerchief knotted tight around his jaw kept him silent. He kicked his legs violently against the edge of the wagon, thinking he might throw himself off the back and perhaps come free from the twine around his wrists and ankles. Instead, he managed only to fall over onto his side, rolling back into the wagon bed.

He couldn't see what happened next.

Henry knew that Tonio had seen him and recognized him the moment he appeared. Now to fade back into the woods and get closer, he thought to himself. He turned and took a step across the *sendera*, crashing right into a large bulky object that grabbed him around his throat. The man who had been in the wagon, having circled through the forest to intercept the young intruder, twisted Henry around and reached two strong arms across his chest and neck. Henry kicked and flailed but without success: the man was much stronger and had him off-balance. Henry writhed furiously, angry at himself for being taken by surprise.

"Settle down, *mi'jo*," the man said in a heavy Mexican accent. "Manuel is going to take care of you now." It sounded to Henry like the man was grinning as he spoke, although he couldn't twist around to see his face.

"Alto!" Manuel shouted, and Henry could hear the creaking wagon come to a stop. The man dragged the protesting teenager onto the trail and the dozen paces until they arrived at the wagon, where Tonio had managed to raise himself onto one elbow. His eyes spoke of the disappointment and frustration that he felt at the moment. In the front of the wagon, the driver on the high bench seat glanced briefly over his shoulder at the proceedings, shrugged his shoulders in boredom, and turned to face down the trail again.

"Are there any others?" Henry asked in a surprisingly matter-of-fact tone. Tonio blinked and shook his head.

"Good," Henry continued. "I'll take this one if you'll get the driver."

"*Silencio!*" Manuel said sharply in Henry's ear, unamused. He bound Henry's hands tightly with a piece of twine commandeered from the wagon bed and threw the boy roughly into the wagon. Henry's legs were free but he couldn't help tumbling onto Tonio who hollered a muffled "Ouch!" The kidnapper hopped onto the wagon himself, skirting the two boys as he moved to the front, and poked the driver in the back as if to prod him into action. Lazily, the driver whistled to the mules and the wagon lurched and moved. The boys were tossed against each other again as the wagon shuffled along the direct road. Henry finally managed to wedge himself against the side of the wagon bed using his untethered legs for balance.

I could jump and run and probably get away, Henry thought, but that won't help Tonio. Best to stay here and be ready, he decided. Besides, he concluded silently, Father will rescue us. Henry looked over at his friend and grinned.

"You have anything to eat? I'm starved." Tonio shut his eyes.

CHAPTER FOURTEEN

Marisol and Crooked Path's mother walked briskly into Nacogdoches, passing the old stone fort on their left and melting into the crowd of people who wandered the hot and dusty main street. No one paid any attention to them as they moved deftly in and around everyone. The Noon sun cast no shadows and any shade on this August day would have been little comfort anyway as the temperature reached into the nineties and the meager breeze blew like a hot breath.

A packed crowd of mostly men had gathered near the center of town. Marisol looked for a way around them but they had filled one side of the street's porches and spilled out into the middle of the avenue. She noticed that the crowd was remarkably quiet, but as they drew near she understood why. A tall Mexican stood head and shoulders above his audience waving his long arms and turning his shoulders as he tried to make eye contact with the men who had gathered around him. Marisol did not care who he was or what he was saying, but neither could she force her way through the packed audience who paid her little heed. Finally, in frustration, the Tejano girl came to a stop, looked at her companion helplessly, and then stared into the crowd looking for a soft spot or gap through which to continue.

Half-listening, Marisol caught part of the man's speech: "-and we cannot afford to let our emotions guide us into violent confrontation with the Mexican government," he said. "Although I share with you the desire to return to the edicts of the Constitution of 1824, we must understand that negotiation with President Santa Anna is our primary recourse, not war. For in war, we will be considered **traitors**," he emphasized the word and paused. "And treason will not further your, that is, our cause."

The men crowded around the speaker and responded with mixed cheers and jeers. Arms waved and pointed into the air and some pushing and shoving went on near the bench where the man stood.

Marisol stood frozen in place as if a giant icicle had just fallen from a barn roof and driven right through her entire body. Icy chills careened up and down her spine and she shivered even as drops of perspiration slid down her neck. She forced her legs to move, although they resisted as if they had been planted in place. She took two steps back from the crowd, glanced at the Tonkawa woman beside her for an instant, and then stared deliberately up over the crowd at the speaker until her eyes met and caught his.

"I know who you are," her lips formed the words without a sound.

Crooked Path ran easily alongside the main road, keeping nearer the trees and the crest of the *real*. He covered the mile and more that Antonio's girlfriend had just run, found where she had stumbled out of the woods, and turned left, vanishing from sight in the shadows. The girl had broken twigs and crushed out a path that he could have followed at midnight, and he needed only to glance ahead to stay on the trail. He passed the disturbed cobweb, noticing indistinctly the huge brown spider already at work repairing the damage. The Tonkawa came to the clearing at an even pace, his breathing still easy, his eyes on the constant look-out. The old lumber road appeared in another moment and Crooked Path turned once more back to the west. Newly-formed wagon marks assured him of his route and he picked up speed as he dashed down the road to where his friends must be.

He had run another mile, perhaps farther before his keen ears picked up the distant rumble of the wagon up ahead. Crooked Path stopped instantly, dropping to his hands and knees and spreading his fingers on the coarse ground. He held his breath and could feel the movement of the wagon vibrating evenly under the surface of the road. Though still out of sight, the wagon was not far away, he decided after a moment's pause.

He let out his breath slowly and came to his feet.

That's when the bear attacked.

"Father!" Marisol spotted him as he stepped out from the edge of the crowd of men off to her right. Even in the noise of the street crowd Señor Calderon recognized his own daughter's voice and he turned in happy surprise. His smile vanished and turned into a serious scowl as he saw her: her hair was wet and tangled, her dress torn and askew, and from twenty feet away he could see the grimy marks of dirt and sweat on her face. His first reaction as he moved toward her was one of anger, but he noticed in her eyes something frightening and he ran the last steps to her side. Without a word at first Marisol fell into her father's embrace, wrapping her arms tightly around his waist as he held her. For a long moment neither moved. Marisol felt a light tap on her shoulder and looked up into the eyes of the Tonkawa woman, remembering.

"Father, something terrible has happened," she began as she looked into his concerned face. The words spilled out too fast and slurred, and her father shook his head and made her stop, pressing one finger gently on her mouth and then brushing a dirty ringlet of hair out of her eyes. "Start over again, little one," he whispered. She did, taking a deep breath and explaining what had happened. When she finished, Crooked Path's mother touched Marisol lovingly on her arm and without a word moved effortlessly through the crowd and disappeared.

Marisol looked into her father's eyes. She said nothing about the speaker they had just heard, but her eyes pleaded for help. "Antonio needs us," she added.

"Bueno," her father replied, still digesting all the information. "Very well, let us go back to the campsite," he said. "We will get the horses and others to help us look for the boys. *Vamanos.*"

They struck out together, pushing their way through the crowd that had now untangled after the lengthy speech. Men in small groups stood around in the Noon heat discussing what they had just heard. Meanwhile, Marisol looked for the speaker over her shoulder. But he had gone.

The young black bear slammed against Crooked Path with its broad shoulder, knocking the boy clear off the road and into the underbrush. Even as he rolled up onto his feet, Crooked Path felt the sudden pain course through his back and neck muscles. The bear continued on its straight path right at him, a permanent snarl on its face. Though not as big as the Indian boy, the young male bear had more than enough strength to win this battle, a fact clear to both of them in that instant. The bear waggled its head as it lumbered across the road, a low growl rumbling somewhere deep inside its throat.

Crooked Path did not hesitate. The knife is already drawn into his right hand and slashed across in front of him in a wide arc, catching the bear across the bridge of its nose and opening a deep cut down its left jowl. Blood spattered into the bear's eyes and onto the boy's wrist as he followed through with his arm swinging around. The bear instinctively lifted its left paw in reaction to the burning sensation caused by the slicing blade, and when it did the momentum of its run at the boy lifted its haunches into the air.

The bear cartwheeled past the boy and into a thorn bush, a thousand sharp points pricking its back and side like porcupine quills. As the bear rolled to a halt in the middle of the bush it let out a horrible squeal as it squirmed to get to its feet. Crooked Path stood in a defiant posture, knife blade extended toward his enemy, but for only an instant. He would not win this fight, not without a prolonged and deadly duel matching blade against claws. Courage in this moment meant using his brains, not his knife!

The Tonkawa boy turned and sprinted to the road without looking back: if the bear followed he would know it.

He raced down the trail, his weapon still drawn, trying to draw even breaths to slow his pounding heartbeat.

The bear, entangled and outraged, only glimpsed the fleeing prey for a moment before returning to the more pressing problem surrounding him. Getting out of this position would take several painful minutes.

Crooked Path ran as if the bear still chased him, pumping his strong legs as he headed for the distant sounds of a wagon carrying his friend Antonio. He stopped only once in the next ten minutes to listen again for the wagon noises and to wipe his bloody blade on a clump of grass before re-sheathing it. The road just ahead of him took a sharp turn to the left and down into a deep dry gulch. He picked up his pace as he followed the trail and a single thought repeated itself as he ran: I will get to Henry Woods and Antonio in time, and Marisol will bring help.

I hope.

CHAPTER FIFTEEN

The pounding hooves beat a steady rhythm on the old Mexican highway that strung out from the town like a wide leather thong. Rough red dirt spewed in all directions as the horses kicked furiously along at their riders' insistence. The mid-afternoon sun shone into eyes that glistened from sweat and grime and the intense heat. The horses ran hard, hastened on by silver spurs digging into their sides with alarm.

Zadock Woods and William Goyens rode ahead of the others, urging their mounts to galloping speed. Just behind, enveloped by the red dust kicked up by the lead horses, Marisol's father and Antonio's father kept up the torrid pace alongside three other men who had volunteered to accompany the search for the kidnapped boys. The posse had dashed through Nacogdoches, sending startled children and squawking chickens scurrying in every direction, and now made their way into the deep woods west of the town, following Marisol's directions.

Goyens, the blacksmith, knew the old timber road well and knew where it headed. If his guess proved correct, they would arrive at the likely hideout in about two hours, skirting the forest trails and staying on the main road. They could also ride up on the kidnappers without being discovered, if - and it was a big chance they were taking - a secret back entry lay unguarded. No one wanted violence, but the boys had to be saved.

The riders did not speak and did not consider the worst possibilities that lay ahead. Caught up in the moment, they rode for all they were worth.

Pitch-black darkness surrounded the two boys with only the tiniest glimmer of sunlight invading through a crack in the wall of their prison. If either boy could have loosened his hands from the ropes that bound them, they would have been unable to see their own fingers in front of their faces. The darkness disoriented them. They lost all sense of time and space, knowing only that they sat tied back to back on a dirt floor in some unknown dungeon.

"Tonio, are you all right?" Henry asked in a whisper.

"Yes, I think so," the Tejano answered weakly. "My eye hurts." His cheek had swollen and discolored where the kidnapper had hit him earlier. Tonio had made a break from the wagon when they had arrived at their mysterious destination along the lumberjack road, but one of the men - the same one that had captured Henry - had run him down and slapped him hard across his face as punishment.

Henry and Tonio had been dragged inside the dilapidated old shack, trussed together with a thick strand of hemp, and tossed unceremoniously onto the floor. The door slammed as the kidnappers left the boys alone - that had been perhaps an hour ago - and now they sat and waited. But wait for what, they each had wondered to themselves.

"I think I can get my hands loose," Henry said simply after a moment's pause. "Can you twist your hands when I do?"

"Si," Tonio replied and began to wriggle his wrists back and forth. The knots were tight and at least three strands of the rope wrapped around the two pairs of hands. The boys sat back to back, another length of the rope girding their

waists, and their ankles had been bound as well. Now they leaned their shoulders hard against each other, working their wrists against the bonds that restricted them. They whispered grunts and groans for the next several minutes, and sweat rolled down their faces and necks as they worked to free themselves. The knot held for the first five minutes without budging at all, and the boys agreed silently to stop for a minute to catch their breaths.

A board squeaked just outside the shack causing both boys to freeze in anticipation. Someone walked up to the door, paused as if to listen for any noises inside, and then seemed to walk away.

Henry waited another full minute before resuming the task, pushing and wiggling every muscle that might help. Tonio dug his heels into the ground as he shoved against his friend's back. Several times they rose right off the ground together and nearly came to their feet before sliding back onto the floor with a thump. The salty perspiration burned in Tonio's swollen eye and he blinked almost constantly to relieve the pain.

But neither gave up the effort: survival meant freeing themselves.

During a second rest period, Henry seemed to sit up straight suddenly as if a thought had just occurred. It had.

"Tonio, I know where we are," he said, tight-lipped and frowning.

"Me, too," Tonio replied with a sarcastic tone in his voice. "We're tied up in the dark in the middle of nowhere, and no one else knows it."

"No, no. Listen," Henry interrupted his friend. "You remember when we came to town last week with our families?"

"Yes," Tonio answered cautiously, recalling the long journey from home to Nacogdoches to attend the fair. "So?"

"Outside of town, on the main road, the ghost town!" He paused. "Bucareli!"

Marisol paced back and forth across the grassy campsite, her hands crossed behind her back as she stamped along in frustration. Her mother watched her from the edge of the tent, not knowing what to say to try to settle her daughter down. Across the camp Minerva Woods sat on the ground, her back straight, idly sewing buttons on a white cotton shirt. Next to her, seeming to keep busy but also watching Marisol pace, Tonio's mother held rosary beads in one hand and mumbled a prayer every few minutes.

The men had ridden off through town to find the lost boys, leaving only Old Wash, Zadock's black servant, behind with the women. The rest of the family who had made the trip were off east in San Augustine horse trading. Marisol had begged to go along to rescue her boyfriend but had been quickly rebuffed by her father. "We will find Tonio and Henry and be back before sundown," he had said just before they rode away.

Now dusk had settled across the busy town and the hot sun turned red as it grew into a huge fiery ball on the horizon. Marisol stopped and looked west into the sun: somewhere out there Tonio was in trouble. Please find him, Father, she said to herself. She put her hands on her hips angrily and kicked a pine cone that had lain innocently at her feet. It bounced across the camp and ricocheted off the side of a tree stump. Señora Calderon raised her eyebrows but said nothing.

Marisol stared at the stump, picturing in her mind's eye Antonio standing on it and waving his hands in a mock speech he had made up two nights before -

That's it! The speech! The speaker! Marisol's eyes brightened as she remembered the man who had been talking to the crowd earlier. She recognized his voice as the one she had heard that night in the forest, the one who had spoken to the others about some conspiracy against the Texans. Traitor. He had used the word in the forest that night and again in his speech. That's what had struck Marisol when she heard it: same word, same voice!

He would know what happened to Antonio.

Marisol hurried to the family's wagon, reaching for a black shawl that lay folded inside and draping it over her shoulders as she headed to the edge of the camp.

"Marisol!" her mother called after her when she realized her daughter was leaving suddenly.

"I'll be right back, *Madre,*" she called over her shoulder, waving her arm in a motion of farewell. "Don't worry. I'll be right back," Marisol repeated as she left the grassy knoll and stepped onto the dusty road that led to town.

CHAPTER SIXTEEN

The knot that had held on so fiercely finally unraveled with a last tug by the boys. Henry slipped his hands out first and quickly turned his attention to the lariat binding his ankles, while Tonio stretched his sore arms for a moment before following Henry's example. The thin leather straps, ordinarily used on heifers at branding time, cut through the boys' pants legs and had already imprinted a reddening line just above their boots. Freed at last, Henry thought better of tossing the thongs, instead stuffing them into his back pocket: you never know when these might come in handy, he thought to himself. Tonio followed suit.

Henry stood up, catching himself against the cobwebbed wall as the dizziness struck him for a few seconds. He hadn't stood for several hours, he guessed. The off-balance feeling passed and Henry stepped silently across the dark room to the door. Kneeling, he could peek through the tiny crack where the last of the day's sunlight still shone through. He spotted part of another building perhaps twenty paces away, and tall fir trees right behind. A hitching post reeled to its side, long since broken and useless. What might have been the stone arch of an old water well could also be seen off to his left? High weeds had grown up in every cranny, and Henry could hear a low hum that seemed to come from just outside and above the door.

"Henry," Tonio whispered from across the shack. "Come look."

Henry crossed the dirt floor and joined his friend at the back wall. Tonio had managed to push away what was left of an old portal cover, and through the small round opening, he now looked out the rear of the building. Tonio stepped aside to let Henry look outside. Three horses lazily stood not ten steps away, tethered to slender boughs that hung from more enormously tall evergreens. Two still carried saddles while a bareback black mare pawed the ground, her tail swishing at annoying flies.

The boys looked at one another in the darkness. No need to speak: they both knew what they had to do.

They split up and moved around the edges of the rundown shack, back toward the front door. When they met, Henry shook his head, but Tonio nodded eagerly and pointed back over his shoulder: he had found a window, boarded and nailed shut but still another escape possibility. Henry leaned his back against the door sill and closed his eyes in thought. Where are the kidnappers, he mulled over the obvious question. If we make a break for the horses, we'll have to go through the door or the side window, cut around behind the shack, and get to the trees. But the men must be around somewhere: how many seconds will we have to get away?

"Let's wait 'til dark," Tonio whispered in Henry's ear, startling him for an instant. Henry opened his eyes, looked in Tonio's direction, and shook his head, No. No time to wait. No telling what their plans are for us. Now or never, he thought.

"Now or never," he repeated out loud just enough for Tonio to hear. Tonio put his hand on his friend's shoulder in response. Henry reached for the rusty iron latch and pushed. The door cracked open!

Marisol walked hurriedly into town looking straight ahead and managing to avoid the still-busy crowds that wandered across her path. She passed the livery and blacksmith shop and the largest of the general stores before she slowed in front of a noisy tavern on her right. Men walked in and out of the swinging half-doors, and the jumble of many conversations poured out onto the street like the mixed smells from an inn's dining room. Without a second thought, the Tejano girl stepped up onto the planked front porch and waited by the entrance. She stood at the edge of the darkening shadows, a flickering kerosene lamp just over her head casting odd dancing shapes on the wall and drawing innocent flying bugs to its deadly flame.

A man appeared at the door, on his way out after his tavern meal. Of average height, he still cast quite a figure in his black, three-piece suit and crisp white shirt. A watch fob dangled from a vest pocket, and a ten-gallon hat hung from one hand, its silver tokens shimmering in the lamplight.

"Excuse me, sir," Marisol spoke as she stepped from the shadows. Her voice was strong and confident and she straightened her shoulders as she addressed the stranger.

"Yes?"

"My name is Marisol Calderon," she said slowly and clearly. The man nodded toward her and waved his hat as part of an informal bow.

"Cap'n James Durst at your service, *Señorita*," he replied.

"Please, sir, I need some help," she said simply.

"What kind of help?" Durst frowned. "Are you in trouble?" He casually looked over her shoulder but no one seemed to be paying any attention to the two of them.

"No sir," she answered. "My friend is in trouble, but my father and the other men have gone looking for him, well, and Henry too, and Antonio's friend Crooked Path has gone but they wouldn't let me go -"

"Whoa, young lady," Durst waved his hat again as he interrupted her rapid explanation. "Now settle down and tell me what's going on. Step over here with me," he motioned, "out of the doorway." They moved down the porch several paces. Marisol sat down on a wooden bench and told Captain Durst what had happened. He listened carefully, interrupting her only twice and asking her to repeat. When she had finished, she stood back up.

"I need to find the man who was speaking today. Do you know where I can find him?"

"Well," Durst paused in thought. "I did see him just a while ago, as a matter of fact. He had a drink in the tavern here, spoke to some of the men who came in, then left." He paused again, remembering. "Took off that away." Durst pointed down the street, then turned and looked straight at Marisol. "But you mustn't go after him. I don't know what all this means, and I can't imagine that he would have anything to do with it. But you have no business chasing him down by yourself, and with night coming on besides." Marisol started to protest but Durst held up his hand. "You stay right here, missy, while I check inside with a friend of mine. We'll see what is going on with all of this. I'll be right back." Durst turned and walked inside the tavern.

Marisol waited impatiently for several minutes. Finally, too anxious to wait any longer, she pulled the shawl up around her shoulders and headed down the street. When Durst and another man returned to the bench, she had disappeared. Durst shrugged his shoulders and made a brief comment about kids, and the two strode across the street toward the hotel.

Marisol picked up her pace again, crossing the rickety wooden porches one at a time as she headed for the western edge of town. She excused herself several times after bumping into people she did not see until too late. Her mind concentrated on only one thing: finding the man who would lead her to Antonio.

There! Up ahead in the shadows, a dark figure walked briskly in the direction of the old stone fort, occasionally glancing over his shoulder to see if anyone followed him. Each time Marisol stopped and leaned into the shadows of the buildings. When he resumed his stride, she followed again. The two followed this pattern until the man suddenly stepped to his right and disappeared from view. Marisol quickened her pace, not wanting to lose him now. When she came to the spot where he had turned off the street, she looked down the dark alley that led to the rear of the old stone fort. Empty.

Marisol stepped into the alley shadows without hesitation. Moving cautiously so as not to stumble or make any noise, she looked for any sign of an open door. Nothing. Two doorways stood along the fort wall but heavy chains crisscrossed the wooden door frames: no one had gone through these doors in a long time, she decided. When she came to the backside of the alleyway, she turned to her left and walked behind the fort.

She paused for just a moment to listen for footsteps but the darkness remained eerily silent. Stepping away from the wall, she peered up to the second story. For an instant, everything seemed deserted. Then a flickering yellow gleam illuminated a window upstairs. Marisol squinted. A silhouette appeared in the window moving slowly from left to right and vanishing with the light as quickly as it had appeared.

Marisol shuddered. Just like that night when she and Antonio had walked here, the dark figure lit by candlelight had moved like a phantom across the second floor of the abandoned building. No ghost, she thought grimly. It's him. And I must make him tell me what had happened to Tonio.

Chapter 16

The girl looked back across the back wall of the fort. Several doorways stood there as possible entries. She tried all of the doors without any luck but started back along the wall to try them again when suddenly a loosened cobweb brushed against her face as it dangled out from the building. Marisol swept the silky strands from her face and stopped. She stared through the shadows at the wall. What had disturbed the spider's web, she wondered silently?

Marisol opened both hands palms-forward to the wall, leaned against the dusty brick surface, and pushed. The wall moved! She pushed again. A secret doorway slid back inside the building revealing a passageway that could not be seen unless someone knew it existed. She stepped inside.

CHAPTER SEVENTEEN

Henry burst through the door, the hinges on the old wooden frame cracking as he stumbled out into the night air. Tonio tumbled out just behind him, grabbing his friend by the arm to regain his balance. Both boys froze in place for an instant, looking in all directions for any sign of the kidnappers. The evening sky displayed every shade of blue imaginable, from the pitch darkness back over their shoulders to the powdery blue on the western horizon where they faced. The sun had not been down for long: they could see across the old abandoned town site. They barely noticed the constant humming just above their heads.

Henry shoved against his friend as they turned to the right to head around the shack where they had seen the horses tied up. Tonio needed no urging as he ran a step ahead. They rounded the corner in three quick strides: the coast was clear!

In that instant, a man stepped from behind the shack. Startled by the two figures coming right at him, the Mexican cowboy stood up straight and took a half-step backward on his heels.

The boys skidded to a stop and turned around in the same motion, racing around to the front of the shack. The man recovered his balance and chased after them, drawing his knife from its sheath as he ran.

"Hey!" he shouted as he ran, loud enough for his voice to echo across into the deep forest that surrounded old Bucareli. Two figures bent over a distant campfire looked up in alarm, reaching for pistols as they stood up.

The man reached the broken front door and stopped. The boys had vanished. He peered inside the dark shack, knife extended in front of him. Suddenly one of them appeared in the thick shadows.

"Don't turn around!" Tonio hollered into the kidnapper's face. The man instinctively disobeyed, turning around to see what lurked behind him.

Henry swung the limb once over his head before he flung it at the man. The makeshift spear flew deliberately

131

high, whipping through the air and striking the top of the door frame with a crunch. The fallen limb split into bouncing twigs as it caromed off the shack. The man dropped the knife to his side and growled a deep, scornful laugh at the feeble attempt of the boy's attack.

The humming noise increased its volume. Henry began to back-peddle across the grassy yard as the red wasps descended on the man, their nest disturbed and hanging now by only a slim thread to the door frame. Angry at being struck by the limb, the deadly insects looked for revenge as they aimed their razor-sharp needles at the man who stood just below. He cried out in panic as the first points penetrated his head and neck, dropping his knife and flailing at the infuriated swarming cloud that enveloped his upper body. They stung his face and throat as he tried to run away; stumbling and falling he disappeared into the woods. The enraged wasps followed like a comet across the sky, a wispy tail of the deadly bugs drifting along after the main horde that engulfed the tortured runner.

Tonio waited one more moment before emerging from the shadows of the old shack. The wasps were gone. He headed for Henry. Movement back over Henry's shoulder! Tonio slowed to a walk as he pointed wordlessly. Henry shot a glimpse behind him. He saw two shadowy figures running from the far side of the ghost town, nearer about twenty paces ahead of the other man. Both moved quickly through the gathering darkness, not running but decreasing the distance between them and the boys with each step.

"C'mon," Henry whispered urgently to his friend. "We can get to the horses." Tonio stole one more glance at the kidnappers before he turned to join Henry. He didn't see the old rain barrel at his feet, tripping ungracefully across it and onto the red soil. A sharp splinter creased his right shin as he fell, and Tonio cried out in pain as he hit the ground hard.

"Henry, wait!" he managed to get out as the ground knocked the breath out of him. Tonio rolled to his right as he grabbed for his bleeding leg. Five steps away, Henry turned to see what had happened. As he took a step toward his fallen friend, a menacing voice rolled across the darkness.

"Hold it right there," the kidnapper ordered. Tonio leaned up on his elbows to see his pursuer. Henry froze in mid-step. The Mexican agent pointed a pistol at Tonio's head from fifteen feet away. Tonio gulped in fear. Henry's eyes widened. The kidnapper grinned without humor and cocked the hammer of his weapon.

The branch of the fir tree rustled only slightly as the figure dropped through the air. Crooked Path landed feet first on the kidnapper's right shoulder, his weight knocking the bigger man off his feet and to one side. His gun popped out of his hand and skittered across the ground. Henry dove across Tonio's prone body and grabbed the pistol just as it came to rest, the hammer still cocked and ready to fire. Henry came up on his knees, both arms extended and two hands holding the weapon pointed at the man on the ground. Crooked Path twisted to his right away from the pointing gun, brushing the pine needles and dirt off his leather vest as he rose quietly to his feet.

"What the -," Henry started as he recognized the person who had come to the rescue. "Crooked Path, how did -"

"Put the pistol down, boy," a gruff voice surprised all three of them as it came out of the darkness. Even the man on the ground jumped at the sound. Manuel Flores emerged from the shadow of the fir tree where only a moment before Crooked Path had pounced. He pointed a shotgun in the general direction of the boys as he spoke, its barrel waving dangerously back and forth as he waited for someone to move. No one moved, not even Flores' partner except as he rubbed his bruised shoulder.

"Put it down, I said," Flores repeated sternly.

Henry considered the desperate situation for just a heartbeat before dropping the pistol into the dirt at his feet. The fallen kidnapper scrambled over to retrieve his weapon, shoving Henry aside roughly as he stood up and backed over to his partner.

"What do we do with them?" the man with the pistol asked.

"They've been too much trouble," came the answer. "And we have no time to waste on them." With that, Flores raised the shotgun to his shoulder and aimed it squarely at Henry's chest. *"Adios,"* he said simply.

Boom! The explosion of the shotgun blast echoed like a stick of dynamite in the night air surrounding Bucareli.

Flores lowered the barrel of his gun and stood absolutely still. He had never pulled the trigger.

"Make just one tiny move for me, Mister, and I'm obliged that it'll be your last on this earth." William Goyens stepped out from behind the shack, the last wisp of smoke coming from the barrel of the gun he held comfortably in both hands. Another figure joined him, a long rifle resting across his chest and in the crook of his arm.

"Father!" Henry shouted.

"H'lo, son," Zadock Woods said with a sly grin, his steely eyes staring through the two startled kidnappers as they raised their hands into the air in surrender. "It's getting late. Didn't want you boys to miss your supper."

CHAPTER EIGHTEEN

Marisol squinted as she tried to see through the darkness of the old stone fort's secret passageway but not a glimmer of light weakened the utter blackness all around her. She raised her hand and felt the grimy wall to her right. Stepping carefully, she slid blindly along the passageway for what seemed like an eternity but was no more than thirty seconds. The passageway turned abruptly at a ninety-degree angle and she turned with it. Another terrifying walk and Marisol's feet stubbed against a raised stone. A stairway.

She made her way up the stairs without a sound, her hand still pushing against the wall. She thought she had counted twelve steps when a brief yellow glimmer silhouetted a door just above. The darkness returned as she climbed the last steps and stood at the door. Marisol listened for any sound from the other side. Everything remained quiet. The man must have walked by with his lantern, she decided. But I can't stay here in the secret passage, she thought to herself.

Cautiously and in slow motion, Marisol placed both hands against the wooden door and pushed, gently at first. It did not budge so she pushed harder. Still nothing. She lowered her hands to her side, rubbing them against her skirt as she thought. Perhaps -

Reaching to the left in the dark, her hand clasped the doorknob. It turned out easily. The latch slipped free and the door swung open just a few inches. Marisol peered through the tiny crack into the room on the other side. Light - moonlight? she wondered - shone from a window somewhere, just barely enough for her to make out the dimensions of the large, empty upstairs room. She listened for a full minute for any sound other than the pounding of her own heart beating. Nothing.

She swung the door open and it creaked angrily. She froze! Another minute passed. No one sprung out at her from the shadows, no other noises could be heard. Stepping silently out into the room, Marisol surveyed the empty space. The window across from her still had several boards nailed against it but at least one plank had rotted away, allowing just a hint of moonlight to seep through. Bits of straw lay without pattern on the wood floor and the large room seemed empty except for two straight-backed chairs that stood face to face in one corner, not far from the window.

Marisol forced herself to walk across the empty space. Fear for her own safety sent a trembling shiver across the back of her shoulders, but she was just as determined to find out about Antonio and that thought kept her courage up.

She knelt beside one of the chairs and picked up a crumpled piece of paper that had been dropped beside one rickety leg. The strong smell of kerosene and the imprint of a man's boots on the dusty floor told her that someone had just been sitting there. Perhaps there had been two, the other, she imagined, sitting across in the other chair as they conspired in secrecy.

But where were they now? She had to find the man she had followed into the stone fort, no matter the danger. Walking around the outside of the room, she came to another doorway she had not noticed before. It led out into a narrow hallway. Marisol crept along the passage. Two locked doors did not budge and did not look like they'd been opened in years. She walked to the end of the hall and into another large room, identical to the one on the opposite side of the building. Her eyes had become adjusted to the darkness but she still could not see into the corners of this empty space.

There, to the right! A door left cracked open! Marisol pushed against the door slowly so as not to cause any more creaking sounds. It swung easily until she could see a tiny storage space through the doorway. She reached for the knob and entered the anteroom.

A large hand snaked around from behind the door and gripped her tiny wrist. Marisol gasped in fright as she tried to pull away, but the viselike grip that held her was too strong. Her soft-soled shoes slid along the dusty floor as the man pulled her into the storage space and slammed the door shut behind them with a *bang!*

Still holding her slender wrist in his huge hand, the man shook her like she was a rag doll. "What do you think you are doing?" he said in a mean whispery voice. "You were following me," he decided out loud. "Why?"

Chapter 18

Marisol couldn't speak. Tears welled up in her eyes and then poured down her face like a waterfall.

"Why?!" The man's voice grew more frightening. He shook her again.

"A-an-Antonio," she sputtered, trying to blink away the tears. "What- have-you-done-with-Antonio?" she said haltingly between sobs. The man bent over and stared into her face only inches away. His expression was terrible.

"*Muchacha,*" he whispered in a voice that sent fear into the pit of her stomach and caused her to hold her breath, "you have no idea what you have gotten yourself into by following me. It is something far greater than you or me or your precious Antonio. It is about rebellion and treason. It is about the end of the pathetic complaints of these Texians and the glory of my *general y presidente* who will soon teach them a lesson." Cordova paused to catch his breath and grinned. "As for you, I cannot allow you to speak of these things, even though no one will believe the crying of a little *Tejaniña.*"

Marisol swallowed. She thought of Antonio, kidnapped and vanished. She thought of her family and her home far away. She remembered the kindness of Crooked Path and his people. She realized she had squeezed her eyes shut in fear and she opened them now. The man's face quivered inches away. Darkness surrounded them. Marisol set her jaw resolutely.

"Believe this!" she whispered into Cordova's angry scowl. Her left hand still free, Marisol swung it across in front of her with all of her strength, her long fingernails scraping across the man's cheek and nose. He yelped like a coyote and grabbed his head with both hands. Marisol grabbed the folds of her skirt with both fists as her right foot lashed out, connecting on top of Cordova's left kneecap. He lost his balance and fell back against the wall of the small room.

Marisol grabbed and turned the doorknob, pulled the door toward her, and leaped through the opening all in one fluid motion. Through the large room, along the narrow hallway, and into the other room she raced, never looking back. She flung the creaky door open and scrambled down the stairs into the secret passageway, somehow keeping her balance as she stumbled down the steps, then right at the

Chapter 18

corner and along the last stretch of the maze until she reached the hidden door that led outside. The fresh night air struck her face as she clambered out into the alley and ran for the main street around the corner of the old stone fort. The salty tears had left grimy streaks down her face, but she did not cry now. Determined to get help, angry and no longer afraid, Marisol ran into the darkened streets of the town and set a course for the safety of the campsite up ahead.

Only the soft beams of moonlight had followed her.

As Marisol raced down the wooden sidewalk passing the hotel, two men stepped out of the wide front doors. Unable to stop quickly enough the teenager struck the man on the right so hard he almost fell to his knees. The other man grabbed both of them by their elbows and lifted them to their feet.

"What in the world, young lady!" the first man barked.

"I'm sorry," Marisol managed in a hoarse whisper, heaving to catch her breath. She looked up at him. And her eyes widened in surprise.

"Captain Durst?" she stuttered.

"Yes, I am," he replied and at the same moment recognized the young girl. "You're the young lady who talked to me earlier this evening."

Marisol nodded, still breathing heavily.

"Are you all right?"

She shook her head.

"Tell me. What's the matter? What's going on?" Durst furrowed his brow in concern as he looked into her eyes.

Marisol squared her shoulders and inhaled slowly to calm herself down. She couldn't think where to begin. Then she remembered. She reached into the pocket of her skirt and retrieved the crumpled paper she had picked up at the fort only minutes earlier. Without a word, she handed it to Durst. The other man looked over the lawman's shoulder as they both silently read what was written. They looked at each other in surprise, then read the note once more.

"It's Cordova," Durst finally spoke. The other man nodded. "And Flores. We've been watching them for days now but had no evidence of what they were up to here in town." He paused and glanced at Marisol with a smile. "But now we know."

"What does that mean?" Marisol asked, unsure what this was all about.

"Well, young lady," Durst replied, "thanks to you finding this note it means we have enough to go after them. This," Durst shook the paper in his hand. "This is a plan to betray everything that many of us here in Texas have been working on for more than a year now."

"I don't understand," Marisol said weakly.

"Cordova and Flores are spies for Mexico City, simple as that," Durst explained. "They're planning a heap of trouble for us, that's for sure. But now we have them."

"They were at the old fort," Marisol blurted out, looking back over her shoulder into the darkness. "I saw them and, well, they saw me. But I got away."

James Durst shook his head. "My, my," he said. "You are something, young lady." He looked back toward the fort. "Betting they're long gone by now." He paused. "But we've got 'em now."

Durst turned to his friend. "Bill, let's get a meeting together first thing in the morning, here at the hotel. Spread the word as much as you can tonight. I'll head over to the sheriff."

"Sure thing, Jim," Bill replied with a nod. And with a polite smile in Marisol's direction, he turned and headed across the street.

"Now, young lady," Durst cleared his throat. "What can I do for you right now? Are you being followed? Are you in danger?"

Marisol thought about the question for a moment. "I'm fine, sir. Thank you. I just need to find my family."

"And where do you think they might be?"

"They're over at the campsite at the edge of town." She pointed as she spoke.

"Well, then," Durst extended his hand to her. "It will be my pleasure to escort you there: the brave young woman who may have saved us all."

CHAPTER NINETEEN
(Three Days later)

The wagons moved slowly down the old Mexican highway, kicking up the red soil of the East Texas ground. Flies congregated around the mules as they pulled the carts in protest. Two goats trailed alongside the third of the four wagons, unconcerned with their surroundings except when a tuft of high prairie grass came into view. The September sun gazed hot and dry from directly above the caravan as the promise of autumn rains seemed an eternity away.

Henry rode his brown mare at an easy gait beside the Calderon wagon. On the driver's bench, Antonio and Marisol sat side by side, the reins held loosely in the boy's hands urging the mules every once in a while. Up ahead the Woods and Gonzalez wagons led the steady pace for the long journey home, while the storage cart brought up the rear. Old Wash whistled to himself and to the gray mule as he followed along.

Exhausted from the adventures that had just concluded, no one spoke very much as they rode along to the southwest. Only at the river crossing did the fresh memories of the danger and excitement revive. There, off to the right in an old clearing, the abandoned buildings of Bucareli looked like a ghost town again. The thick underbrush and prairie weeds seemed poised to reclaim the area as if no one had ever lived there. As if nothing had ever happened there! Henry smiled. His friends smiled back.

EPILOGUE

September 18, 1835

Sixteen-year-old Henry Woods sat at the edge of his front porch at the fort listening with complete attention as his father read the newspaper that had just been delivered by a courier from San Felipe.

Next to Henry sat his oldest brother Norman. In the rocking chair next to his father's sat Minerva Cottle Woods, and in her lap rested one of Henry's little cousins, brother Monte's youngest daughter.

It was Henry's father's sixty-second birthday and the rest of the large family would soon be arriving at the fort to celebrate the occasion. Several neighboring families would also be showing up in time for the big birthday supper.

But Zadock Woods, his long white hair gently bobbing on his shoulders in the gentle breeze, had a stern look on his face as he read the headline news.

"What is it, Pa?" Henry asked.

"It's a speech by Colonel Austin, sure is," the old Indian fighter said with a respectful tone. "Listen to this, everyone."

Zadock drew the circular closer to his face and began to read:

The Texas Republican. September 13th, Eighteen Hunnert and Thirty-five. Col. Stephen F. Austin, our most respected leader in Texas, has at last safely returned to our fair country after two years illegally imprisoned in Mexico by the dictator Santa Anna. He is well and has this to say to the citizens of Texas: War is our only resource. There is no other remedy but to defend our rights, ourselves, and our country by force of arms. To do this, we must unite.

THE END

Next, the great adventure of Henry Woods and his companions in the exciting conclusion to these tales of the Texas Frontier:

Book Four: FOUR DAYS AT GONZALES

And

Book Five: THE CANNON AT GONZALES

Made in the USA
Coppell, TX
27 September 2024

37760923R00090